February's Regrets
A Larry Macklin Mystery-Book 4

A. E. Howe

Books in the Larry Macklin Mystery Series:

November's Past (Book 1)

December's Secrets (Book 2)

January's Betrayal (Book 3)

February's Regrets (Book 4)

March's Luck (Book 5)

April's Desires (Book 6)

May's Danger (Book 7)

DEDICATION

For the men and women of law enforcement—
especially those of the Tallahassee Police Department and
the Leon County Sheriff's Office, many of whom I've had
the privilege to work with and call friends.

CHAPTER ONE

I looked out the window onto my frozen twenty acres and thought, *Could there be a worse month to be unemployed than February?* All I wanted to do was crawl back into bed. Ivy, my adopted tabby cat, looked at me as though she thought anyone who got out of bed to do anything but eat and do their business was an idiot. She was enjoying my unemployment and thought I should just spend every day scratching her and dispensing treats.

"Not this morning, girlie. I need to find a real job to keep us in frosted flakes and cat food." She mewed and rubbed against me. "Enjoy," I said, pushing my cereal bowl over to her so that she could lick the last bit of milk from the bottom.

While it had been almost a month since I had handed in my resignation, it had only been a week since my last day working full time for the Adams County Sheriff's Office. It had taken that long to finish up the paperwork on the murders, rapes and attempted killing of the sheriff that had led me to hand in my notice. It hadn't helped that we'd been assisted by the Florida Department of Law Enforcement and the Drug Enforcement Agency, adding untold levels of bureaucracy to the reports.

At the request of the sheriff, who also happened to be my father, I was still a reserve deputy with the department, but I didn't plan on working any more hours than necessary to maintain that status. All of which begged the question of what I was going to do now.

At least the sun was out, giving me enough motivation to push back from the kitchen table and get dressed. I'd just managed to put on pants and a shirt when there was a knock at the front door. Since my property was about five miles from town, it was odd that someone would be visiting me out of the blue on a Tuesday morning. *Jehovah's Witnesses or Baptists?* I wondered as I went to the door.

"Hey there, Mr. Brighteyes," Shantel Williams said when I opened the door. Shantel was one of the best crime scene techs in the department and a friend.

"What are you doing here?" I asked, surprised.

"Freezing my patootie off. You going to invite me in?" Her smile was forced. Normally she was the type of person who was always on the verge of laughter, but she seemed distracted this morning.

"Yeah, yeah, come in."

She followed me into the living room and I suddenly noticed how filthy the place was.

"I see you're settling into unemployment," she teased, but again the humor seemed more out of habit than part of her normal good spirits.

"Are you okay?" I asked, concerned.

"Let me sit down." She took a seat on the sofa, shifting a pile of books out of her way.

Shantel had only been out to my place once before, to drop me off when my car was in the garage, so I knew she was there for a reason. I had to resist the urge to bombard her with questions, giving her time to get her thoughts together.

"I need your help." Before she could stop it, a tear rolled down her dark brown cheek. She wiped it away in irritation.

"Anything," I said and meant it. When I'd gone to work

for the sheriff's office, Shantel had been quick to give me advice and to help me learn how to preserve and search a crime scene. Once I became an investigator, I quickly learned that Shantel and her partner, Marcus Brown, were the best assets I had in the field. Not that Shantel wasn't quick to let me know if I did something stupid. She did that with everyone and didn't care who she might piss off. She wouldn't tolerate fools.

"My niece, Tonya, is missing."

I remembered seeing a couple pictures on her desk. One of them was of a smiling, lanky woman in a graduation gown.

"From Adams County?"

"Yeah. She lives over on King Street and people saw her Saturday night. But she's just gone. She texts me every day. Dumb stuff, but every day. Nothing since Saturday."

I'd never seen Shantel this rattled. Usually she was the boss in any room. If I had been the type to give hugs easily I would have gone over to her, but I wasn't so I just sat across from her, feeling helpless.

"Have you talked with anyone at the department?"

I saw a spark of the old Shantel when she gave me a look that was a mix of irritation and frustration. "Of course I talked to Pete. But you know we're four deputies short. Your father's going crazy because he can't afford the overtime." She threw me an accusing look, then went on. "Pete took all the information, but he's got a pile of cases on his desk. And... Tonya's life has been a bit mixed up since she graduated from high school."

"How old is she?"

"Twenty. She got into some trouble when she went to community college in Tallahassee. Partying too much. It got a little scary, but I went and brought her home. She's been doing well since then. Can't get a job, but no more drugs or alcohol."

"You know I quit."

"I know you're still a reserve deputy. And you're the best

7

investigator we have… had."

I was pretty sure she was just flattering me to get some help.

"I…"

"Your dad will let you take the case if you ask."

That was a conversation I didn't really want to have "Before we do anything desperate like talk to my father, let me look into it. Maybe there's a simple explanation. Did you take the day off?"

"I couldn't go to work today. I drove around most of last night looking for her car. I've worked for the department for fifteen years… I know that people go missing all the time and show back up. People do weird crap that their families never thought they'd do. I *know* that. And I pray that's the case here. But I'm scared." She dropped her gaze to the floor.

"Something else is going on. What do you know?"

Shantel sighed. "I know something I shouldn't."

I just looked at her, puzzled.

"I was over in Tallahassee last week and stopped by to see a friend at the sheriff's office there. I'm not saying who 'cause it wasn't their fault. I was in their office and they left to take care of some business. I was bored and there was a file on the desk. I admit it. I'm a snoop sometimes. I got to looking at it." She just stopped talking.

"What was in it?" I prompted.

"You can't tell anyone I told you this."

"What?"

"Promise. 'Cause if it got around, my friend could be fired."

"I promise," I said, a bit exasperated. "Now what did you see?"

Shantel sighed heavily. "I'm probably worrying for no reason. But…" She paused for so long that I thought I'd have to prod her again, but she finally went on. "The file was on a murder case that Leon County is investigating. When I opened it there was a picture of a young black girl, and she looked so much like Tonya that I almost dropped the thing."

"But this was before Tonya went missing?" I was a little confused. The fact that I was entertaining a visitor before ten o'clock in the morning wasn't helping.

"That's right. I looked at the file a lot closer then… This is the terrifying part. It's a Swamp Hacker case."

I felt my stomach heave and my breathing grew rapid. "Not possible. It must have been an old file… or someone's messing with you."

"They haven't made anything public yet. But I know what I saw. There were the cuts on the back. Just like…" Shantel stopped, near tears again. I'd never seen her this close to the edge. We'd worked a hundred accidents and murders together, including a gruesome body found in a hot tub the month before. She was always a rock of emotional stability when others were choked up or throwing up.

"And then Tonya went missing," I said for her.

She nodded. "You're the only one I've told about the Leon County case. Leaking information on an active murder case, even to you, is a crime. That kind of screw up could get me fired at the very least. I never should have been snooping," she chastised herself.

"Even if it is a new Hacker case, it can't have anything to do with Tonya."

"All of his victims came from here," Shantel reminded me.

"But only one of the bodies was found in Adams County," I said.

"Yeah, the rest were left in swamps in Leon or Jefferson County. You were how old back then?"

"Fifteen. You know, I saw Sierra Randal's body." My mind went back to that day in January sixteen years ago.

"How'd you manage that?"

"I was in high school and had joined the journalism club, so I was staying after a lot and didn't always come home on the bus. Dad picked me up that day. He'd just become an investigator in October. When he drove up in the unmarked car, I thought it was so cool… and funny as hell to see him working in a jacket and tie. Halfway home he got a call about a body that was found just inside the county line. Dad being Dad, he told me we were going to the scene. It was only his second murder investigation."

"Taking a boy to a murder scene," Shantel said, shaking her head, but I knew she wasn't surprised. My father could be incredibly single-minded and a bit clueless.

"I was thrilled. I thought that this was my chance to be a real reporter. Of course, when we got there, Dad ordered me to stay in the car. We were parked about a quarter mile from the body. They'd already figured that this case was related to the others in Leon County and were determined to preserve any tire prints or other evidence the killer might have left behind."

"How long did you wait in the car?" she asked.

"About five minutes after Dad was out of sight. I followed the road up to where Dad and the other deputies were looking around for tracks and other obvious evidence. They were waiting on forensics and the sheriff. I don't know what the hell I thought I was doing, but I walked to the side of the dirt road. Everyone was looking at a spot about twenty feet on the other side of the ditch. The ground was wet and mucky. I remember it was warm for a winter's day."

"No one stopped you?"

"I just walked up like it was the most normal thing in the world for me to do. Most of them were too captivated by the body to notice me. Even from there you could see the horrible slashes across her back. I don't know what I imagined a dead body would look like, but this was horrible. I wanted to go help her. She looked so alone. I think I even started to move toward her, but then I felt a hand grab the back of my coat."

"Don't have to tell me who that was." Shantel smiled a little.

"He pulled me halfway back to the car. I heard words that he normally reserved for lawnmowers that wouldn't start."

Shantel shook her heard. "I didn't see my first murder victim until I was almost thirty."

"It definitely made an impression on me, but I think the weeks and months afterward when Dad was trying to find the killer made an even bigger impression. He was so intent on catching the Hacker that we hardly saw him for months. Of course, he had to spend a lot of time in Leon County with the task force, but it was more than that. I think he personally interviewed every witness in Adams County, and he sat in on most of the interviews in Leon too."

"The last body was found in April."

"Dad stayed on the case full time through the summer. When the sheriff reassigned him, Dad refused to quit and worked during his off hours for another couple of months before Mom convinced him that he had to let it go."

"I remember all us single girls being scared to death to be alone at night. Even if there were a couple of us, we'd get a guy we trusted to go with us if we were going out. And when they found the couple murdered in the swamp, I just refused to go anywhere at night for weeks. Guy or no guy," Shantel stated.

"Of course, none of the murders were actually committed in the swamp. I remember how mad Dad was every time a newspaper or TV reporter called the murderer the Swamp Hacker. He didn't even kill them by hacking them."

"That's right, he hit them on the head. Oh, my God." Shantel put her hand up to her mouth.

I realized I'd forgotten the reason Shantel came to me. "I'm sure Tonya is fine."

"Help me find her, Larry," she pleaded.

"I'll do what I can." I didn't believe that Tonya could be a victim of the Hacker. I didn't really believe that he could be back. If he was, it was going to be a shock to a lot of people. I had no idea how Dad would react. I wanted to give him a heads-up, but Shantel was right. She could have been fired for what she'd already done. The leak had to stop with us. The LCSO would have to give out the news soon enough. They couldn't sit on the story forever.

"What can we do?" Shantel seemed so lost. It was a reminder that even the strongest person can be dealt a body blow.

"First, let's forget the Leon County murder. Even if it is the same murderer, there's no evidence that it has anything to do with Tonya. We're just going to tackle this like we would any missing person."

"I've talked to everyone I can think of and I've been working on a timeline." Shantel seemed to get a little of her old determination back, pulling up the timeline on her phone.

"Great. I want to copy it and we'll start working on a plan for today," I said, getting up and digging for a notepad.

After making notes from the timeline, I asked, "This is Saturday. What did she do Friday?" I knew we'd have to work further and further back if we didn't hit on anything right away.

"She spent all day Friday looking for work. She'd had jobs in Tallahassee, several, when she was in college, but just entry-level stuff and, with her partying, she'd either quit or been let go after a couple of months. And, yes, I know how this sounds. But she was just like every other kid who goes to college, gets in over their head and flunks out the first year. She'd taken it to heart. Tonya really wants to make good. She's applied to just about every business here in the county."

"Must have been hard."

"She seemed okay. Maybe a little down, but determined."

"Does she have a boyfriend?"

"Nothing steady. She's only had one serious boyfriend, but he went to work out in North Dakota and she went to college. That's when they drifted apart. Since high school, she's just had a few guy friends, but nothing serious. I'd have known. There was nothing she liked better than telling me every detail of her social life. That girl can talk. If she went out on a date, I'd get a couple of pictures before it was even over. She did all that Twitter, Facebook and Snap-whatever stuff… But there's been nothing for days."

"What about her parents?"

"Tonya was raised by my momma. She's worried sick too. But, honestly, Momma's pretty clueless. My sister died of a drug overdose ten years ago. She'd never taken care of Tonya. No idea who the daddy is."

I realized how little I knew of Shantel's life. I knew that most of her family lived in Adams County, though she'd spent part of her childhood in Savannah when her father was in the military. But I'd only recently learned that she'd been married and divorced. How can we work with people, call them our friends, and yet know so little about their real lives? I felt like I hadn't been much of a friend.

I stood up. "Let's split up and interview as many people as possible. Did Pete put out a BOLO on her car?"

"Oh, yeah. Pete knew he wasn't going to get rid of me without doing that at least." She shook her head. "The car has to be here someplace. It's so old and broken down, I don't think it can make it out of the county."

CHAPTER TWO

I started with a list of almost a dozen people and possible job search locations. I planned to get through as many of them as possible, regardless of whether Shantel had already talked with them or not. A pair of fresh eyes and ears wouldn't hurt. Shantel headed out to put some pressure on some of Tonya's friends and family to start taking a more active role in looking for her.

On the off chance that you might strike gold on the first try, it's common practice to start with a missing person's last known location or contact, then work backward. First on my list was Jenny Caroll, Tonya's friend since middle school and the last person Shantel knew for sure had been with her.

I pulled up to the daycare where Jenny worked. Shantel had called ahead and told her to expect me. When I got out of my car, I realized how odd it felt going to interview someone in my own car and without my badge. I had to keep reminding myself that this wasn't official business. I' was just playing private eye for the moment. With luck, we'd either find Tonya or have enough evidence to convince the sheriff's department to make her disappearance a priority.

Jenny left her terrifying minions in someone else's care and came outside to talk to me. "I told her auntie that I don't know where Tonya is," she said, a little too quickly.

"We're trying to trace all of her movements Saturday night, and I'd like to get a sense of her mood. What did she talk about?"

"We just hung out for an hour." Jenny shrugged.

"What'd you do?"

"You know, like, hung out."

There are times I despair for the younger generation. We'd have to do this the hard way. "Where did you hang out?"

"My boyfriend's place." Nothing more. Some interviews were like pulling teeth.

"Where's your boyfriend's place?"

"I don't know, north side of town. Like, he's got a trailer up there," Jenny said, waving her hand in a southerly direction.

"I know you all were hanging out, but what were you doing?" I didn't want to mention any specific activity, such as watching TV, because I was sure she'd say, *Yeah, watching TV.*

"Are you, like, a real cop?"

"Yes, I'm a real deputy, but I'm not on duty right now. I'm helping out Ms. Williams. She's a friend of mine like Tonya's a friend of yours," I reminded her. "You don't seem very concerned?" I made it a question, hoping to draw more out of her.

"Well... I don't know," she said.

People let her watch their kids? I wondered.

"What don't you know?" I tried to press her.

"It's just... She wanted to do some stuff, she needed money, but, like, she knew her aunt wouldn't like her doing them," she rambled.

"I need to know what you're talking about. All her aunt and I care about is that Tonya is safe. Once we know she's safe, we won't be pestering her friends anymore. And, to be clear, by pestering I mean coming over to their boyfriend's house unexpectedly and looking around to see what kind of trouble I can cause him." I hoped that a none-too-subtle threat might make some impression and help Jenny focus.

"Yeah, well, okay, I guess. She couldn't find work. Like, nothing, and she really, really tried. I tried to get her on here," Jenny indicated the daycare, "but she'd been arrested in Tallahassee and had a minor drug thing on her record so she couldn't pass the background check. Stupid."

I shook my head, but probably not for the reason she thought. There was a long pause, then Jenny finally said, "She thought she might be able to get work at the Sweet Spot."

My heart sped up. The Sweet Spot was a booze-and-whatever joint that the sheriff's office was constantly trying to close down. It had been shuttered for a couple of weeks after the owner, Justin Thompson, was arrested by the DEA. But a few transfer-of-ownership papers later and it was back open. You'd have to be pretty naïve to believe that it was really under new management. It was a very bad sign if Tonya had gone there looking for work. The place usually employed a couple of women to show cleavage and encourage the men to drink. The joint also served as a place for men who were looking for companionship to find women who were looking for cash.

"When was she going to the Sweet Spot?"

"Jerry, my boyfriend, gave her a hard time. Like, told her that she didn't have big enough… breasts to work there. He got her real mad and she said she was going there right away. Wanted me to come, but I didn't want to. She kind of left, you know, in a pissy mood."

"You think she went straight there? What time was it?" I couldn't believe what an airhead this woman was.

"Yeah… Nine maybe?"

An older woman stuck her head out the door. "Jenny, you need to get your butt back in here and watch some of these kids." The woman apparently knew the addle-headed Jenny well because she added, "Now!"

Jenny frowned at me.

"Go on, but if you think of anything else, call me." I handed her one of my cards. I was still waiting on new ones reflecting my reserve status, but what Jenny didn't know wouldn't hurt her. "The sooner we find Tonya, the sooner we quit bothering you."

"Jeez, she probably just got a job and didn't want her aunt to know. Gawd. You know, I care too." She turned and stomped back into the daycare.

There were more people on my list and another fellow I wanted to chat with, but Jenny's news about the Sweet Spot made it the top priority. Going there without a badge and backup was stupid, but I couldn't wait. I needed someone to know where I was headed and my only real choice was Shantel. I called her as I started driving.

"I'm going around to the Sweet Spot. I just wanted you to know in case you don't hear from me for a couple of months." I tried to make a joke, but we both knew it wasn't funny.

"Why?" I heard the puzzlement in Shantel's voice. I wasn't going to tell her that Tonya might have gone there Saturday night. Not until I'd had a chance to check it out. The last thing I needed was an angry aunt kicking down the walls.

"I want to talk to someone," I said, leaving it very vague.

"Do you think that's a good idea?"

No, I thought. But aloud I said, "The Thompsons don't own the place anymore," not believing it for a minute.

"Every one of them are out on bail except for Justin, and he's perfectly capable of running things from his county jail cell."

"It's eleven o'clock in the morning. I'll be fine." There was some truth to that. There were places and streets that were deadly after midnight, but were perfectly safe before noon.

"Well, what's the lead?"

"I'll call you in an hour. If you don't hear from me, send lawyers, guns and money," I answered and hung up before

A. E. HOWE

she could ask any more questions.

The parking lot of the Sweet Spot was a horseshoe of grass and dirt surrounding a garishly painted cinderblock building. I pulled in and parked as close to the front door as I could. Two other cars were parked nearby. Both of them looked like mid-level management for the drug trade—nice rims on crappy cars.

I got out and looked around. I wasn't wearing my badge, but I did have my gun, concealed by law since I wasn't on duty. Tougher to get to if needed, but if I needed it in the Sweet Spot it probably wouldn't matter where I was carrying it.

I stepped inside the building and let the door close behind me. It was very dark—the only windows had been painted over years ago. I stood there, letting my eyes adjust to the dim light. There was one man behind the bar, another picking up trash and putting it in a bag and two men seated with their backs against the far wall. No one was over thirty and they all looked like life had run them over several times. Stale beer and urine competed for the strongest odor.

"Mister, you got the wrong bar," the man behind the counter told me.

"No, I don't."

"Oh, shit," said one of the men against the wall. "That's the sheriff's son."

"You definitely have the wrong bar," the bartender told me.

"I've got a few questions and then you can go back to business as usual."

"Hell, no," the bartender said. He was tall with broad shoulders, but a thin waist. In the dark of the bar I couldn't make out his features.

"You might want to reconsider that answer," I told him.

"They'd fire my ass if I talked to you," he said with certainty.

"Whoever owns this building probably doesn't want any more crap coming down on them right now." I moved toward him so he knew I wasn't intimidated. "There's a girl missing. I want to ask a few questions and get a few honest answers. Once that's done I'll walk out the door and everything goes back to normal. But if you stonewall me, I'll see how much trouble we can bring down on this joint, making damn sure that your bosses know you could have stopped it."

One of the men with his back to the wall cackled. The man picking up trash hadn't looked up since I came in and now I noticed that he was wearing earbuds, the cord running to his phone.

"Bullshit," the bartender said.

"I'm Larry Macklin," I said, as though introducing myself at a party.

He didn't say a word.

"The polite thing would be for you to give me your name."

The bartender looked over at the men against the wall. They both shrugged. "Who are you looking for?" the bartender asked me. Progress.

Reluctantly I went over to the bar, putting myself farther away from the door. I carefully reached into my pocket and brought out my phone. Shantel had sent me a couple pictures and a short video of Tonya. I pulled up one of the pictures and turned the phone to the man.

"Her name's Tonya Williams."

He made the classic mistake of looking up at me from the picture. I could tell that he recognized her. Now he was trying to figure out what to tell me. "The truth," I suggested.

"She's been here. So what?" He was trying to play it tough for the audience.

"When? Was she with anyone?"

"Been here a couple of times with some guy. Knew they were trouble," he grumbled.

"Why?"

"'Cause they didn't belong here. Should have been gettin' ice cream or some shit. Asked stupid questions and didn't know nothin'," he said, sounding disgusted at their naiveté.

"Was she here Saturday night?"

The bartender paused, thinking about his answer. "Yes. Stupid tail wanted a job. I told her this wasn't damn Walmart or some crap. She wouldn't take no for an answer. Saturday night, we're busy, I didn't have time for that. She hung around and hung around until some old-timer grabbed her tender parts. She got all offended and ran out."

"Oh, hell, I remember that," said one of the men against the wall. He started to laugh. "First piece of anything ol' Ray's gotten in years." This caused the other man to laugh too.

The man collecting trash seemed to realize he was being left out of a joke and took out his earbuds. "What?" he asked loudly, causing the other men to laugh harder.

"Did you see her or hear anything else about her after she left?"

"No, nothing. Like I said, it was Saturday night. It was busy."

"What time did she run out?"

"How the hell…" he started to say and then saw the hard look in my eyes. "Maybe eleven? Best I can do."

I turned to walk out.

"I can tell you one more thing. If she hung around outside on a Saturday night, she'd get more than a little groping from Ray," he said to my back. I felt my face flush. With my blood growing hot, I stalked out of the bar.

CHAPTER THREE

I drove around the neighborhood for a bit to see if Tonya's car was parked somewhere near the Sweet Spot. Nothing. Giving up, I looked at the clock on the dash. It was noon so I called my girlfriend, Cara Laursen, and offered to take her to Winston's Grill for lunch. Then I dialed Shantel.

"I survived."

"What was that all about? Don't you dare say nothing."

"I'll tell you when I see you. Let's meet about three o'clock in the parking lot of the Walgreens. Have *you* had any luck?"

"I've got some family and friends beating the bushes. No one's heard from her. But some of them are finally getting concerned."

"We'll find her." Why do we promise things like that when so much is beyond our control?

As we ate lunch, Cara filled me in on her morning spent with the dogs and cats of Adams County. She worked at Dr. Barnhill's clinic as a vet tech. I loved listening to her prattle on about the clients and their animals. We'd only been dating for a few months, and I wondered if the glow I felt watching and listening to her was something that would wear off in time. I hoped not.

"Not looking for work," I responded cheerily when she asked me what I'd been up to.

"Okay, that's not good," she said, but with a laugh in her voice. She came from a family of modern hippies, and jobs and money were not her highest priorities.

"Shantel's niece is missing. Shantel came by this morning and asked if I would help look for her."

"Missing? How old is she?"

I gave her all the details, making the trip to the Sweet Spot sound a bit more causal than it was.

"Poor Shantel. So you're like a private detective now?" Cara asked with a mischievous smile.

"Never," I said firmly.

"Never say never."

"Being a private detective would require that I be a good detective and a good businessman. I'm neither. Plus, you'd have to be a snoop."

"I'm snoop enough for both of us," she laughed.

"You're enjoying this. I'm out of work and you're having a good time at my expense."

"It's going to be funny right up to the point that you and Ivy get foreclosed on and you all have to come live with Alvin and me." Alvin was her Pug.

"I can think of worse things," I said suggestively. "We could have lots of... fun."

"We can do all of that without the horror of actually cohabitating."

I thought for a minute. "Fair enough."

After I dropped Cara off at the vet, I drove out to Albert Griffin's place. Mr. Griffin was the county's unofficial official historian. He ran the local historical society and had taken over the newspaper's morgue when it went out of business, archiving many county and city records that would otherwise have been discarded.

I knocked on his door, wondering if I should have called

first, but the robust old man smiled brightly when he opened the door.

"Macklin, first name, Larry," he greeted me. "You were here back in November when there was all that trouble."

"That's right, Mr. Griffin." He made me feel like a ten year-old talking to my teacher.

"Come on in. That cold air doesn't do any good for these old bones," he said, ushering me in. The house was filled with books and papers. The odor was that of an old bookstore and cats.

"What can I do for you today? I heard about that business at the parade last month. The world gets crazier and crazier." I was following him into the living room, but he stopped in the doorway and turned back to me. "I say that, but there have been wild things taking place in this county going back to the first settlers. I'm sure that the Creek and Cherokee, and the Apalachee before them, would all have their stories to tell. No, people don't change much."

I had to rearrange some papers and displace a cat to find a seat in the living room. This particular feline was a playful black-and-white kittenish thing. I didn't see the large black tom who'd tried to stare me down during my last visit.

"I'm looking for information on the Swamp Hacker," I explained. The thought that he might be back had been eating at me. I'd come to Mr. Griffin because I couldn't pull any files at the department without attracting attention. He was my next best option.

"The Hacker." He shuddered. "Dark times. Our own version of the Zodiac, Son of Sam or the Texarkana Killer. For months we became the town that dreaded sundown." He got quiet, lost in his own thoughts. Then his eyes came back to me. "Why are you interested in him now?"

"I don't know if you heard or not, but I resigned from the department after the trouble at the parade."

"No, I didn't. Sorry to hear that. You seem like just the type of man who should be in law enforcement." He sounded sincere.

"I appreciate that, but there's too much water under that bridge. Anyway, I've got some time and I thought I might write an article on the Hacker," I said, making up a story as I went along.

"Excellent!" Mr. Griffin's face lit up. "I've said for years that someone should write a book about the murders. It's probably not even a downside for a book that he was never caught. How many books have been written about the Zodiac or Jack the Ripper? Wow, where to start? I guess you should tell me what you need. Do you have access to the police records?"

"Only those that are available to the public. It's still an open case."

"Of course it is."

"Maybe I can start with some questions."

"Wait! I remember your father was the lead investigator from Adams County. That's right. Though the task force and the authority was with the Leon County Sheriff's Office. No wonder you're interested in the case. Ask me anything." He opened his arms wide.

I knew quite a bit about the cases, but I still had a lot of questions. "There were six bodies found over a six-month period. The one in Adams County was the fourth one, right?" I asked.

"You know, I have some notes around here someplace and a scrapbook of the murders that an old woman gave me. Be right back." He got up and hurried off through the piles. I hoped I'd be that spry when I reached his age.

I felt a dozen needles pierce my ankle. "Ouch!" Looking down, I saw two black-and-white paws slapping at my shoelaces. I played with the prickly monster until Mr. Griffin came back.

"He has been a menace since he got here." Mr. Griffin looked down and frowned good-naturedly at the spastic little creature still clawing at my laces. Suddenly the kitten quit playing and ran out of the room. The black cat with the fierce eyes I'd seen the last time came in through another door and sat frowning at the place where the kitten had been.

"About time you got here, Brutus. You need to take a firmer hand with that youngster." Mr. Griffin turned to me. "Without my cats, the mice would have reduced my archives to confetti long ago."

He sat back down in his chair and put the scrapbook and an old yellow legal pad on his lap. "Now I'm ready. Where were we? The bodies. The first one was discovered in November. Let me see…" He flipped a couple of pages in his yellow pad. "On the twentieth of November, the authorities got an anonymous tip. When a Leon County Sheriff's deputy responded, they found the body of Tara Dunaway in a swamp near Tallahassee. Right before Thanksgiving. Not much was made of it at first. The body'd been out there for a week so the hack marks weren't as blatant. It wasn't until the first of December that they knew she'd been taken from Adams County."

"They never found a murder site," I mused.

"That's right. Speculation at the time was that he clubbed them to death and then used a pickup truck to transport the bodies to the dumpsites."

"Was the hacking done when they were murdered or when the bodies were dumped?"

"That's information you'll have to get from the autopsy reports. There was a lot of information that they never released. Not because the reporters didn't ask." He tapped the thick scrapbook.

"The second and third bodies were discovered in mid-December, right?"

"That's right. And the publicity around the cases started to go crazy. Jim Merrell and Tiffany Falls, college students. He was white, she was black. Also, those bodies were found by a hunter only a day after they were placed in the swamp just off a main road. With the cool weather and the fact that they'd only been out there a day, the wounds from the cleaver were very obvious. Connections were made back to

25

the previous murder and the papers and TV proudly announced that there was a serial killer on the prowl."

"They were from Adams County too."

"Exactly. Which put the bull's-eye squarely on us. The two victims had gone to Adams County High School and a lot of people knew them. The fact that it happened right before Christmas didn't help. Lots of memorials and vigils."

Mr. Griffin opened up the scrapbook and flipped to the front. He turned it so that I could see two front-page newspaper articles. Pictures of the victims showed happy, good-looking kids. Below their pictures were photos of flowers and crime scenes. One headline read: "Who's Hunting Us?"

"Is that your scrapbook?" I asked.

"Oh, no. I was given this by Mary Dolan."

"The sheriff's wife?" Richard Dolan had been the sheriff of Adams County from 1984 to 2008. I'd known him and his wife well.

"She gave it to me about two years ago, just before she died. Richard had passed away the year before. Mary broke down and cried when she entrusted me with this scrapbook." He ran his hand over the binding. "She told me that she'd started it after the fourth victim was found. She wanted to have a record of the case so that when Richard solved it, someone would be able to write a book or make a movie about it. Richard himself could never let it go. According to Mary, this case was one of the last things he talked about when he was in hospice care. Very sad."

"A case like this affects a lot of peoples' lives." I thought of my own family. How might our lives have been different? Even with the passage of time, I knew that Dad still returned to the case from time to time.

"Now things got very interesting. The fourth body was found here in Adams County. Sierra Randal was discovered at the end of a dirt road near the county line. In fact, the road crosses the line at one point and then re-crosses it." I saw the scene clearly in my mind's eye. How much of what I remembered was reality and how much had my mind embellished over the years?

"You were how old?" he asked as though he'd read my mind.

"Fifteen."

"I imagine you remember it pretty well. Especially since your dad was so involved. People truly lost their minds. The sheriff put a curfew in effect and had extra patrols out every night. What added to the terror was that no one knew where the victims were killed or where they'd been abducted from. People didn't know what or where to avoid or who should be afraid. The answer seemed to be everyone. At least everyone under the age of thirty or who cared for someone under the age of thirty."

"Kayne Stone was the next victim," I recalled.

"Yep. A twenty-seven-year-old African American who'd moved here with his family when he was a teenager. Here was a strong, healthy guy who, like everyone else, knew that there was a serial killer on the prowl and still he was killed. A fact that did not make anyone feel better."

"His body was actually found in Jefferson County."

"But still in a swamp. Everyone wondered if the killer had been forced to change the type of victim and dumping location because of all the stepped-up measures of law enforcement."

"And the citizen groups. I remember all the landowners, hikers and hunters being told to be on the lookout for anything strange in the woods. Dad had to run down hundreds of tips."

"Obviously nobody knows for sure why he changed his pattern. Maybe he just wanted to bring in a whole 'nother group of law enforcement officers and panic another county. We'll probably never know. What we do know is that he skipped March and killed his last victim, Erika Sykes, in April, a week after Easter."

"I remember people talking about the fact that he started a week before Thanksgiving and ended a week after Easter."

"That's right. Some folks thought he ought to be called the Holiday Killer. Kind of a double meaning there, 'cause he sure killed most of the holidays for folks that year. But some reporter at the *Democrat* dubbed him the Swamp Hacker after the second and third bodies were found and nothing was going to rid us of that hyperbole."

"Dad hated that name." I remembered him cursing under his breath every time someone used it.

"And, of course, he bashed them to death rather than hacking them to death. But no one has ever accused journalists of being slaves to the truth."

"Dad always hoped to find the blunt object that was used." Every time they had a suspect, he'd tag and bag anything that might have been the murder weapon. It must have driven the labs crazy.

"There must have been a tremendous amount of pressure on your dad." Again, Mr. Griffin read my thoughts.

"Most of it was placed there by his own sense of duty. He never felt pressure from the sheriff. In fact, I know Sheriff Dolan did everything he could to help Dad and to take the burden of responsibility onto his own shoulders."

"Two honorable men stuck in a trap not of their own making. The world can be a cruel place."

I glanced at my watch. I would need to leave soon if I was going to meet Shantel on time. "Mr. Griffin, I've got a meeting at three. Could I borrow the scrapbook?"

He looked down at it and seemed to consider my request. Then he slowly offered the book to me. "Take care of it and bring it back as soon as you're done."

"I will."

"I'd like to read your article when you're done. You should really think about writing a book about the case."

I nodded. I'd almost forgotten the white lie I'd told. Maybe it wasn't a lie. Maybe the last chapters of the book were being written as we spoke.

CHAPTER FOUR

I'd chosen the Walgreens parking lot because it was far enough away from the sheriff's office that we shouldn't run into anyone else from the department. I didn't want to get into a how's-it-going meeting right now.

Shantel was waiting for me when I got there. She was standing by my car before I even had a chance to turn it off. "What have you found?" she asked, hanging in the window as the cold air blew around her.

"Nothing much. Get in the car and we'll figure out our next move."

After she was seated, I told her what I'd found out about Tonya and the Sweet Spot.

"No. No way she'd go there. By herself on a Saturday night? I don't believe it. Let's go talk to Jenny and find out why she's lying," Shantel said through clenched teeth.

"She wasn't lying. She's no Mensa candidate. I'm not sure she'd be capable of telling a convincing lie. I've met lots of folks who could lie straight to my face and I wouldn't have a clue. She's not one of them."

"What are you saying?" It spoke to how upset Shantel was that she needed to be walked through this.

"You need to consider the fact that Tonya had a life of her own and that she didn't always do the right thing or the smart thing."

Shantel thought about it for a few moments. "I know I was a bit blind to what she was getting up to in Tallahassee, but to go to the Sweet Spot? Lord, what was she thinking?" Her voice was pleading.

"Tonya loves you a lot. And she wouldn't want you to be disappointed in her or to disapprove of her choices. That's going to make this a little harder than it might otherwise be. But you can make it easier, and possibly help to find her faster, if you think about her more as an independent person. If I have to fight you to get you to see the truth, it's just going to slow us down."

"Tonya is a good girl," Shantel said, staring at me with eyes that were dark and challenging.

"I'm not saying she isn't. If she was bad, she wouldn't care what you thought of her and you wouldn't find this so hard to believe."

Shantel considered this for a minute. Finally, still not happy, she said, "Okay."

"So we're good?" I pressed her. Another beat passed before she nodded her head. "Then what you need to do is call Pete. We need to have a look at any calls for service to the Sweet Spot or in the surrounding area Saturday night." I paused. "I can't call because I'm not officially working this case. Pete thinks a lot of you. He'll get us what we need."

She called him and Pete agreed to pull the information. He had already opened a case on Tonya and the information was public record anyway.

"He's going to meet us at Winston's in half an hour."

I had mixed feelings about seeing him. Pete Henley was my best friend in the department and had been my partner, but he was very miffed when I resigned without talking to him first. I hadn't seen him at all since I'd stopped working full time.

Shantel and I took a seat in the back of Winston's. The dinner crowd was still an hour away, so there were only half a dozen people talking and eating.

Pete shook his head and frowned when he saw me sitting with Shantel. "I hope you just bumped into him," he told her.

"He's helping me look for Tonya," she answered.

"I'd be able to work on it on the clock if we weren't so short-handed," he said, still standing and looking pointedly down at me.

"You can't blame me for Matt, Edwards and Nichols. My resignation is my business," I defended myself.

"You didn't resign, you quit," Pete shot back. For a man who almost never got angry, he could do it well when he wanted to.

"Can we just work on finding my niece. Please!" Shantel hissed at us. Ashamed, Pete and I broke eye contact with each other and he dropped his nearly three-hundred-pound frame into a chair beside us.

A waitress I didn't recognize, but who clearly knew Pete, came over to the table with a cup of coffee for him. The older woman then turned to us as though we had appeared out of thin air. The reception for Pete was not surprising since he made Winston's his office away from the office, but it still made me feel like a poor relative. Hadn't I left a full twenty percent at lunch?

After Pete ordered a piece of pie, he pulled a couple folded papers out of his jacket pocket. "There were the usual public nuisance calls, a report of gunfire, and one of the patrol deputies nabbed a guy for public indecency. Nothing unusual for Saturday night at the Sweet Spot. Actually, it's been quieter around there since the Thompsons were hauled in."

I looked at the reports. None of them seemed to point toward Tonya. Deputy Julio Ortiz was the deputy on the wienie-waving report. I made a note to get in touch with him. Since it hadn't been a call for service, it meant that Ortiz witnessed the suspect breaking the law, which meant he'd already been at the Sweet Spot looking around. The time on the arrest report was eleven-thirty, half an hour after the bartender said that Tonya was groped by the old man. She might still have been close to the bar. The rest of the reports occurred either before or hours after the time that Tonya was seen there.

Pete ate his pie and we filled him in on what we'd been doing.

"I'm not going to give you a hard time for sticking your nose in this," he told me.

"Gee, thanks, sir," I said a little too sarcastically, but he took it well.

"It's just unlucky that some asshole quit his job so that I'm busy as hell doing his work as well as my own. Seriously, I feel like crap that I can't jump on this." He turned to Shantel. "Tonya's probably fine. You know the statistics—almost all missing persons are missing because they want to be."

Shantel shook her head. "She would have called or texted."

"We can get the cell phone company to check the pings coming from her cell phone."

"Please. I don't know what I'm going to do if we don't find her soon."

"I'll do it as soon as I get back to the office," he said, cramming the last bite of pie in his mouth and standing up before he swallowed. "I better get back. Did I mention that we're snowed under?"

"Who are they going to move up to investigations?" I asked.

"I'm more concerned about when. But they are advertising three patrol positions and one investigator position. So it looks like they're going to promote one deputy and hire another experienced investigator from outside the department. That ought to be fun. But who knows? Your dad might change his mind." Pete dropped a ten on the table and left.

"What do you think?" Shantel asked, sounding tired and looking apprehensive.

"We just have to keep knocking on doors. If you can put more pressure on friends and family, all the better."

"I don't know how I can stand another night not knowing where she is."

"Let's go find this boy she went to the Sweet Spot with," I said, which had the desired effect. Shantel's eyes lit up with anger.

"Nothing I'd like better." She stood up and I touched her arm.

"Listen, when we find him, you can't go in there with guns blazing. We need to come at him from an angle. You with me?"

"Whatever you say," Shantel said flippantly.

I locked eyes with her. "I'm serious. We can't go crazy. Remember, you may need his cooperation."

"I understand." This time she sounded more serious, but I still had my doubts that she'd be able to control her temper.

"We'll leave your car here and go together," I told her.

CHAPTER FIVE

Shantel dialed around Tonya's circle of friends until she found someone that would give up the boy.

"His name is Jarvis Monroe." She gave me his address, which was in the same historically black neighborhood where Shantel lived. "He's just two blocks behind my place, and I've never met him. How could Tonya be seeing some boy from the neighborhood and not bring him by?" Shantel was talking more to herself than to me.

Cara called as I was driving. "I got off a little early. Do you want me to come over? I can bring something for dinner."

Yes, I thought, *I want that very much.* Aloud I said, "Shantel and I are still out talking to folks. If you want to go on to my place, you can feed Ivy and I'll be there just as soon as we get done." On an emotional high after we'd survived a rough patch in our relationship last month, I'd given Cara her own key to my place a few weeks ago.

"Ivy and I probably need some girl bonding time anyway," she said good-naturedly.

I promised to call as soon as I was headed her way.

The day was beginning to fade and the temperature had dropped by the time we found the small, shotgun-style house where Jarvis lived. The house was painted in bright blues and greens, and the front porch was wrapped in plastic to winterize it.

I parked on the street rather than block the narrow driveway. The yard was hard-packed dirt with neatly organized flowerbeds lying dormant. I knocked on the outer porch door, but it was evident that no one in the house would be able to hear the knocking over the sound of a loud TV. I opened the door and we stepped onto the porch and into a veritable jungle of potted plants. I recognized some— spider lilies and philodendrons—but others were a mystery. I knocked as loud as I could on the interior door, trying to be forceful enough to be heard without sounding like a raiding party.

The door was opened by a tall, thin young man with a boyish face. He was wearing an FSU sweatshirt and jeans that barely clung to his butt.

"Yeah?" he confronted me, trying too hard to look tough. He failed miserably. Shantel was standing behind me and, when he caught sight of her, his eyes went wide.

"I've seen you," Shantel said accusingly.

"Oh, man." He almost moaned the words. "You're her auntie. Where's Tonya? I'm going crazy." He seemed very upset. His hands never stopped moving as he rambled. "I haven't heard from her since Saturday. It's not like her. I know we're not like boyfriend and girlfriend, but we're close, man, and she doesn't leave me hanging—"

I raised my voice over him. "Stop. Stop. We're here looking for her."

"Don't tell us you don't know where she is," Shantel said, accusation in her voice. All of the fear and anxiety that she'd been trying to control for days was ready to come roaring out as anger as soon as she found a suitable target. I had to make sure she didn't take aim at Jarvis without cause.

"Let's calm down and go inside where we can talk," I told both of them.

"Man, ain't no room inside. Grams is watching her

shows. The only way you can stand it is to have buds in." He indicated the earbuds hanging around his neck.

"We can sit in the car," I suggested.

"No, no. The neighbors see me talking to you, they'll think all kinds of crazy stuff and tell Grams." Jarvis thought for a moment. "We can go around back."

He led the way off the porch and we followed him down a narrow path between his grandmother's house and the neighbor's. We went through a gate and were instantly greeted by an overly affectionate grey Pitbull who tried to lick and jump on all three of us at the same time.

Jarvis opened the door to the back porch and fetched the dog's food. He filled up a bowl while talking baby talk to the dog, who ate up the attention as ardently as the food.

"We can sit there," Jarvis said, pointing to an outdoor table and chairs.

"Jarvis, we know that you and Tonya went to the Sweet Spot together a couple of times. Tell us why you went there and what happened while you were there."

"Oh, damn," he said, rubbing his head and face with his hands. "It was just a thing. She was all like, 'You're so nice, Jarvis, you're too sweet, don't you ever do anything exciting?' So I was like, 'Okay, I can do something. I'll take you to the Sweet Spot.' She liked that. Tonya kinda liked the gangsta thing. But she'd got in trouble in Tallahassee, so she was really trying to stay clean. I think that's why she wanted to hang out with me. But she got bored, I guess. That's why I took her to the Sweet Spot. 'Cause I was afraid she was going to get tired of being with me. But where is she now?" His voice cracked a little with this last question.

"How could you take her there?" Shantel asked, as much to herself as to him. She'd apparently decided that he wasn't a strong enough target for her anger.

"I shouldn't have. After we went there the first time, that's all she'd talk about. Could I take her back? When could we go? I didn't want to hear about it anymore, but she kept on. Finally we went back. Mostly she just wanted to be there. We drank some beers and watched people. Oh, yeah, we were pestered by the dealers. You can't sit there for two minutes without someone trying to sell you something, I didn't like it."

The young man prattled on so much that it was hard to get a question in. Finally I just blurted out, "Why there?"

"What?" he asked after I'd gotten his attention.

"Why the Sweet Spot? Why not someplace in Tallahassee?" The Sweet Spot wasn't really a place for college-aged kids, even ones looking for trouble. Its main clientele were older men and women who were looking for a fix *now*. Probably half the people there on a Saturday night were there because they didn't have transportation to someplace better.

"My uncle hangs out there a lot. Some of the older guys hang out at his house. I know 'em."

"So you felt safe there." I made a note to pay the bartender back some day. He and everyone else in the bar had known who Jarvis was, but none of them were going to make it easy for me. Maybe someday I'd have the opportunity to chose whether or not to make something easy or hard for the bartender. It wasn't going to be a difficult choice.

"Did you notice anyone looking at Tonya?"

"Everyone looks at Tonya. She's hot," he said, not disrespectfully, but I saw Shantel stiffen and her eyes blaze.

"But did anyone look at Tonya more than the others?" I persisted.

"No. I don't think so."

"Did she talk to anyone in particular while you were there?"

Jarvis seemed to think for a minute, then shook his head.

"Did you know that she went to the Sweet Spot on Saturday night?"

"This Saturday?" He seemed surprised.

"Yes, this Saturday."

"But she was with her friend Jenny," he said, not a shred

of doubt in his voice.

"Did you talk to her or text her Saturday?"

"Yeah."

"Can I see your phone?"

"Are you, like, a cop?" he asked.

I needed to tread lightly here. I didn't suspect him of harming Tonya or knowingly being involved in hurting her, but he was naïve enough that someone else might have used him to lure Tonya into something bad. I didn't want to taint evidence by pretending to be working on the case. I decided on full disclosure.

"I'm a reserve deputy with the sheriff's office, but I'm not here in an official capacity. I'm just trying to help my friend, Tonya's aunt. We just want to get her home safe. You seem like a nice guy who cares a lot about Tonya. Letting us read her messages might help us to figure out where she is, and how we can help her." I used the most reasonable tone I could muster. Jarvis really did seem like a good guy and, most of the time, appealing to someone's good nature is not a bad way to start.

"I guess. But I've read them like a million times. And she doesn't say much except she had a plan to get work." Jarvis pulled out his phone and handed it to me.

As I scrolled through their messages, I angled the phone so that Shantel could read along. The messages ran the gamut: arranging to meet; Tonya complaining about someone or something; Tonya ecstatic over clothes or food. Jarvis mostly responded to Tonya with a little not-so-subtle flirting that she deflected.

Tonya: *Bored!*

Jarvis: *What's you doing?*

Tonya: *With Jenny and her boyfriend. he's an ass.*

Jarvis: *We could do something. Want to meet?*

Tonya: *Got to get a job!!!!!!!!!*

Jarvis: *yeah*

Tonya: *No one wants to hire me when they find out I got in trouble in Tally!*

Jarvis: *There must be someone who wouldn't care.*

There was a few minutes' pause before Tonya responded with: *Got an idea! Why am I so brilliant?!!!*

Jarvis: *What's the plan? Can I help?*

Tonya: *Got to check it out first. Tell you when I see you!*

Jarvis: *K.*

And that was all there was except for a dozen messages from Jarvis asking where she was and if she was okay. I checked his recent calls and there were several from him that only lasted a second and no incoming calls from Tonya. I handed the phone back to him.

"Why are you asking about the Sweet Spot?" Jarvis asked.

I thought about my answer for a minute. In an interview you always need to make sure that, if you give out information, it's for a reason. The question was, would telling Jarvis that Tonya went to the Sweet Spot serve any useful purpose? Looking at the sad young man sitting in front of us, I decided that we needed an ally who had a different perspective on Tonya's life than Shantel did.

"She went to the Sweet Spot looking for work," I told him and his eyes got huge.

"That's crazy. The girls that work there… Oh, no. Why'd she do that?" He stood up and started pacing back and forth. "Man, is this because I took her there? Oh, man."

I felt Shantel shift, but she didn't say anything. I'd been worried that she might pile guilt on top of Jarvis over this, but it was clear that while he may have made some bad decisions, he really did care about Tonya.

"The decision to go back to the Sweet Spot was her own. You can't blame yourself. What we need is for you to calm down and help us find her," I told him.

He remained standing, but stopped the manic pacing. "What can I do? Anything."

"Obviously, I don't know all of her friends," Shantel said. "I need you to write down the names and numbers of all the friends you know. If you can, call them and ask if they've seen her or know of other friends or places she might go."

"Okay, yeah, I can do that." It was obvious that he was looking forward to doing something to help find Tonya.

I pulled a pen and paper out of my pocket. In the dim light cast from the house, Jarvis wrote down a dozen names, about half of which were unfamiliar to Shantel. As soon as he was done writing, he got on his phone and started making calls.

While Jarvis contacted Tonya's friends, I called dispatch at the sheriff's office to get a number for Deputy Julio Ortiz. When I reached him, he told me he was going on duty in about an hour and agreed to meet with us. We left Jarvis with the assurance that we'd let him know when we found Tonya. I hoped it was a promise we'd be able to keep.

CHAPTER SIX

It was fully dark by the time we rendezvoused with Deputy Ortiz. Tall and lean, his vest, belt, radio, gun and other equipment appeared to cling to him like climbers scaling a peak.

"Hey, man, you working tonight?" he asked me. I'd already done a couple of shifts on the road this month to maintain my reserve status.

"No, I'm helping out Shantel. Her niece is missing."

"Hey, Shantel, sorry to hear that. That's rough. You think I can help?"

"Maybe. We know that she was over at the Sweet Spot on Saturday about the time that you cited a guy for public indecency. We just wanted to pick your brain. See if you remember anything."

"The Sweet Spot." You could almost hear Julio thinking, *What the hell was she doing there?* "I remember. Guy pissing in the street. Drunk. Everyone outside that place is high on something."

Shantel pulled up a good picture of Tonya on her phone and turned it to him. "Taken last week. I don't know what she was wearing Saturday night."

"Hmmm, I don't know. I had a few minutes between

calls, was in the area and decided to drive by. There were some guys standing outside. Maybe half a dozen, all of them looking suspicious. They got real interested in their feet when they saw me. But then I noticed this joker standing between a couple of cars, pissing in the dirt. He was swaying back and forth, too drunk to even know I was there. I would have just given him a citation, but he was too drunk to leave. I put him in the back of my car. A miracle that he didn't puke."

"Did you see any women?"

"Maybe. When I was leaving I was in a hurry because I didn't want the guy to hurl in the back of my car. But a house or two down the street, I saw a person walking across a yard. Might have been a woman. It was dark and half the streetlights around there are busted. I thought there was something odd about the person, but nothing was obviously wrong. Nothing said this could be a problem. Not like the drunk in the back of my car."

Julio gave me specific details regarding which yard he saw the person in, though he admitted it could have been a woman *or* a man, then headed back to work.

"I can go by there in the morning," I told Shantel.

"We can go now," she shot back.

"Shantel, it's getting late and the neighborhood—"

"No, I understand," she said.

I sighed. "Okay, we can go, but if I get shot it's your fault."

"No one's going to shoot you. Besides, now's the best time to go there. People are more likely to be home." I don't know who she was trying to convince, but I understood why she couldn't let it go.

I called Cara to apologize for being late. She was continuing her long-standing campaign to make friends with Ivy.

"I'd have an easier time getting close to an A-list movie star," she grumbled.

"She's a bit of a prima donna," I admitted.

"Well, if she wants some of the chicken I brought then she's going to have to make nice. Speaking of chicken, have you had dinner?" As soon as she said it my stomach growled.

"No. And I'm starving." I looked over at Shantel, who rolled her eyes. "You have to be hungry too," I said to her, holding the phone away from my mouth.

"Are you going to be much longer?" Cara asked.

I looked over at Shantel. "Hard to say. We're checking out one more lead. I'll know more after that. I'll call you."

Shantel handed me a PowerBar that she'd found in the console. "Mind if I have one?" she asked.

"Please, eat. I don't want you passing out on me." I tried to kid her, but jokes just weren't very funny today.

We drove past the Sweet Spot, which looked fairly quiet this early on a weeknight. I pulled over across the street from the bar and just short of the house that Ortiz had indicated, turning off the headlights.

Shantel reached for her door, but I put my hand on her arm.

"Not yet. I want to watch the house for a few minutes first." She nodded and settled back in her seat to watch with me.

The house was concrete block, featureless and with no more than eleven hundred square feet. Lights were on in the front windows. We saw someone walk through the living room, but nothing more. After fifteen minutes I figured we'd learned all we could from the outside.

We dodged deadfall and various trash as we walked across the yard to the front door. We were lucky that there was enough light coming from the house for us to avoid most of the junk. Up close, it was obvious that the house hadn't been painted in a decade. The front door was a cheap, hollow-core interior door. *At least we can be sure that whoever lives here isn't dealing drugs*, I thought. I made sure that Shantel was close enough that anyone looking out from inside would

43

see her too. I thought that would increase the chances that the occupant would open the door.

I knocked. Nothing. I knocked again. Still nothing. The third time I heard someone approach the door. I could feel whoever was on the other side of the door looking us over.

"What?" came a voice from inside.

"Could we talk to you for a minute?" Shantel asked in her friendliest tone.

"Got drink, don't need your god, go away," was the charming reply.

I dug into my wallet and pulled out a twenty, a ten and a couple of fives and held them up so they could be seen through the DIY peephole in the door. "We just have a couple questions. If you have really good answers, there could be more," I told the door.

After a short wait for the alcoholic on the other side of the door to consider how much Mad Dog 20/20 could be bought with forty dollars, we heard the chain on the door slide back. The chain was a waste. I could have put my fist through the door.

A grizzled old man, his gray three-day growth of beard contrasting sharply with his dark oak skin, peered out at us suspiciously. Then, to my surprise, he stepped out onto the stoop with us, pulling the door shut behind him. We were all uncomfortably close on the four-by-four concrete slab. I stepped back off of it to escape the stench of alcohol sweat coming off of him. A second later Shantel joined me.

"What you want? You ain't cops," he told us. I wasn't sure why he didn't think we were cops, but if it made him feel better, he could go on believing it.

"What's your name?" I asked, although I'd already looked it up on the property appraiser's website.

"Ra'," he said, sending spittle flying. His full name was Raymond Emery, so close enough. I handed him a five-dollar bill, which he snatched and crammed into his pocket.

"Were you home on Saturday?"

"No. Gimme my money." His toothless mouth would

have slurred the words with or without the alcohol.

"I said a couple questions. Where were you?" I tried to keep my voice light and easy, trying to sound more like an MC on a quiz show and less like the cop he'd told me I wasn't.

He looked at me like I'd asked him to calculate the time of the next full lunar eclipse in the southern hemisphere. "Why you want to know?" he finally asked, slowly and suspiciously.

"Not the way the game works. I ask the questions and you answer. Get the answers right and you get money. Now, where were you Saturday night?"

"I don't remember. I was drunk." I was sure that the first statement was a lie and equally sure that the second statement was the truth.

"Guess we don't have anything more to talk about," I said and started to turn.

"Give me my money." He tried to grab me, but was too slow and too drunk.

"One last chance. Want the money? Then where were you?"

"He was at the Sweet Spot," Shantel said, causing both of us to turn and look at her. "You don't have to give this saucepot forty bucks for something I can tell you."

"How you know that?" he slurred in her general direction.

"The Spot is the closest booze hole. Where else would an old booze hound be on a Saturday night?"

"Ha, you ain't so stupid," he said to Shantel and then turned to me. "Now give me my money."

I held up the remaining thirty-five dollars and handed it to Shantel.

"Hey! What the…"

"She's the one who told me where you were. Now go to bed."

"No, wait…" he blathered, then changed his mind. "You bastards get off my property!"

"We're going," I told him.

Shantel made eye contact with me and I shook my head no. She was puzzled, but followed me as I walked back to the car. The drunk stood on his porch, swaying in the cold night air as he watched us leave.

"Why didn't you ask him about Tonya?" Shantel sounded a bit upset.

"Because he's hiding something and I can't force him to tell me. At least not yet. I'm going to drive around for a few minutes to give him a chance to go back inside and forget we were here. Don't worry, we aren't done with ol' Ray." I didn't tell her that he had groped Tonya in the bar on Saturday. I didn't want her to have a stroke.

We were back in five minutes. I approached from the same direction as before, thinking that he might have decided to take his five dollars and wander over to the Sweet Spot, but we didn't see him. I certainly wasn't worried about him seeing us. At night, at his age, and in his state of permanent intoxication, the chances he could see more than five feet in front of himself were nil.

I parked a little farther away from his house this time, just in case he mustered enough paranoia to look out the window. The lights were still on in his house. After a few minutes, we saw him stumble past the front windows, probably in the living room. No doubt he was on his way to the bathroom to drain his bladder or to the kitchen to fill it up. His life's work.

"Why are we watching the house?" Shantel was agitated. She needed a reason to be sitting there staring at a house when she wanted to be out looking for her niece.

"The bartender at the Sweet Spot said that a guy he called ol' Ray was there Saturday night when Tonya came in." I left out the details.

"You should have asked him about it." Shantel was not interested in subtleties right now.

"He barely gave us his name, and he didn't want to admit that he was at the Sweet Spot. Why not? Because he has something to hide. If I was on duty and could take him down to the office for questioning, maybe."

Shantel started to speak, but I held up my hand. "And if we don't find out anything by watching him for a while, we'll find some way to take him in and put a little pressure on him."

We killed half an hour with texts. Shantel went back and forth with several of Tonya's friends, including Jarvis. Everyone had been out looking for her, but no one had found or heard anything. I checked in with Cara, letting her know it was okay to give up on me and go home.

Finally I decided we'd wasted enough time. "I'm going to walk around his house." I pulled out a small LED flashlight and checked it.

"Not without me," Shantel insisted.

"Just wait here, I won't be that long," I told her.

She wasn't having any of it. "I'm going."

"Two of us are more likely to be seen. I just want to check the windows. See if I can tell why he obviously didn't want us in the house. I might find something that could give us leverage to pull him in," I tried to reason with her.

"You forget. I'm the crime scene tech. You rely on me to find evidence. I am just as good at seeing things as you are."

I'd seen her like this before and never once had she backed down when she'd staked out her ground. I sighed. "Fine. But I'm not letting you use my flashlight."

"Got my own," she said, pulling a similar flashlight out of her coat pocket.

We got out of the car and snuck across the street. Since the yard hadn't been maintained, there were plenty of bushes to use to conceal ourselves as we made our way to the house. I was counting on Ray's lack of sobriety to work in our favor. Once up against the house, the trick was not to stumble over any of the trash strewn about. We had to be careful using our flashlights. We didn't want one of the neighbors to call 911 thinking we were prowlers just because we were prowling.

The cheap windows were in aluminum frames and most of them didn't have curtains on the inside. Going around the south side of the house first, we passed a bedroom that did have curtains, but they were parted enough so we could see the filthy conditions of the room. I swear I could smell it from outside. A double bed on a metal frame took up the center of the room, while a couple of cheap dressers were scattered along the walls. The next window was small and made of frosted glass—clearly a bathroom.

The kitchen was in the back of the house. Light from the living room filtered in and, knowing that Ray probably made frequent trips to get beer or wine, I didn't want to linger at the window.

Things got strange when we came to the next window past the kitchen, which I'd figured was for a small bedroom on the northwest corner of the house.

"Interesting," I whispered to Shantel.

"What?" she whispered back, coming up alongside me.

"It's painted—" That's as far as I got before the old wooden privacy fence running along that side of the property was rammed by something large and aggressive from the other side. The roar of barking exploded in our ears.

"Shit, run!" I hissed to Shantel. She started to go forward. "No, no, back the way we came," I told her, half pushing her.

We hustled as fast as we could back around the house, then hunkered down in the bushes across the street from my car. We didn't dare cross the street after all that ruckus. If anyone was watching, they would have easily spotted us.

Apparently the neighborhood was used to the barking dog because no neighbor appeared to look out a window or open a door. Strangely, though, Ray came out and stumbled around his house, paying very special attention to the side next to the privacy fence.

CHAPTER SEVEN

Ten minutes later we were back in the car.

"Jesus," Shantel said, holding her hand over her heart. It wasn't an exclamation, but a prayer.

"The window of that bedroom was painted over," I told her.

"Drugs?" she asked. It wasn't unusual for people growing pot to paint and/or cover their windows with foil so that they could run grow lights without anyone noticing the glow.

"That old man? Pretty unlikely."

"Person that lived there before him?"

"Believe it or not, he owns the place and has for twenty years. Maybe a family member. But we didn't see or hear anyone else. No cars in the driveway."

"Larry, I've got to find Tonya. Drugs or whatever he's doing, I don't see where that helps us to find her."

"I don't know if it does, but there is something weird going on with him."

"So what?" Shantel asked as I was trying to figure that out.

"I'm going to call Julio. He can come by and talk to Ray. See where that gets us. Maybe Julio can talk himself into the house."

"Can Julio take him in for questioning?"

"One thing at a time. I know you're anxious, but we can only go so fast without screwing things up. If you want, I can take you back to your car and Julio and I will deal with Ray the drunk."

"No, it's all right. I can't think of anything else I could be doing right now except driving around looking for her car. And I spent hours doing that already. I'll see this through."

I nodded and took out my phone. It was twenty minutes before Julio returned my call.

"Sorry, man, I was on a domestic. Nasty one. Two ladies. A girl-on-girl thing. Had to call in backup. What can I do for you?"

I explained the situation.

"Hey, you're not an investigator no more. I don't have to take your orders," he kidded me. "Let me check in with dispatch. You say this is an open case?"

"I don't want to get you in trouble. I'll give Pete a call and clear it with him."

"I'm not questioning you. Just, you know, Major Parks doesn't want us doing favors," he said, referring to the department's head of human services and resident curmudgeon.

"I understand. Get dispatch to clear you and I'll call you back."

I didn't want to call Pete, but I was also sure that Pete would be glad to okay it. I got him on the first ring.

"It's after ten. What's going on?" Pete was a solid guy. He knew that if I called him at home at this hour it had to be important. I explained the situation to him.

"Oh, hell. Okay, listen to me. I'm coming out there. Don't do anything until I get there. You need to either get on the clock or stand way back," he told me. Being a reserve officer was not the same thing as being a full-time deputy. If something went wrong, there could be a lot of questions as to why an off-duty reserve officer was on the scene.

"Look, you don't need to come out here. This is probably

nothing. I was planning on letting Julio take the lead."

"Shantel is my friend too. I feel shitty for not being able to put her niece's case on the front burner. I'm coming out. Actually…" He paused. "I'm glad you agreed to help her. I'll be there in thirty."

I called Julio and told him we were clear, and he confirmed that dispatch had assigned him. My next call was to the duty officer. We were short-handed so a sergeant was on duty, which was good. I had a better chance of bluffing a sergeant than one of the lieutenants.

"You're working a case?" Sergeant Toomey sounded suspicious. "You're a reserve officer now," he reminded me.

"I was just checking something out, but now the witness looks like he's developing into a case himself."

"Anyone authorize your hours?"

"I'll cut back somewhere else. Promise. I won't ruin the department's budget."

"Okay, I'll put you on at ten-thirty. Call me directly when you're going off the clock."

"This shouldn't take long. I'll call you when it's over," I said, thinking that had gone smoother than I expected.

Julio and Pete showed up together. Pete had parked down the street to avoid having too many cars show up in front of Ray's house.

"You want me to try and get in the house and check out the room on the northwest corner. Got it," Julio said.

"And if he won't cooperate, tell him we need to question him on the disappearance of Tonya Williams. If he's unwilling to talk voluntarily, then go ahead and take him as a material witness," I told Julio.

"You know, if you hadn't resigned you could be working this case," Pete said. To Julio, he said, "Do what he says."

"Anything else we can do for you?" Pete asked. Could his voice have gotten any more sarcastic? I cut him some slack since I had dragged him out of his house after ten at night.

"You could call me and put your phone on speaker so I can hear what's going on," I said, smiling. Pete just frowned back at me.

"You two are fighting like an old married couple. I don't think the separation is working," Julio said, getting out of his cruiser.

Shantel and I sat in my car across the street and watched Pete and Julio walk up to the house. My phone rang.

"I hope you enjoy the show," Pete said. I put my phone on speaker so Shantel could listen.

"You really think this has something to do with Tonya?" Shantel asked me.

"I think we need to follow this lead as far as it will go. If it doesn't pan out, we'll move on," I told her. She frowned, but settled back in her seat to watch and listen.

Julio walked up to the front door with Pete in tow. We heard the knock on the door and Julio shout, "Sheriff, open up!" More knocking. "I know you're on the other side of the door. Open the door so we can talk."

The door opened. "What?" slurred Ray. We could see how unsteady he was from our vantage point across the street. He was even more drunk than when we had talked to him.

"I need to check out your house," Julio bluffed. Ray was within his legal rights to refuse, but a surprising number of people, even ones with something to hide, can be bluffed out of their rights.

"No!" Ray said.

"Then we'll need you to come down to the office to answer a few questions," Julio told him.

"What for?"

"Sir, if we could just take a look around." We could see Julio step forward. I was surprised that he was able to withstand the odor enveloping ol' Ray. It was an excellent tactic. A lot of folks will involuntarily step back, giving you access. But not Ray. He stood his ground.

"Youdon'tneedtogointhere," he slurred, and that was when Ray made a mistake. He put his hand on Julio. Julio grabbed Ray's hand, but Ray was quicker than I would have thought possible and managed to evade Julio's grasp. That's when he made his second mistake. He turned to go back into the house. If he had been arrested out on the lawn, Julio would still not have had a right to enter his house. But since Ray "assaulted" the deputy and then fled into the house, Julio had every right under the law to pursue him.

I got out of the car and jogged across the street. The reason for me to hang back was so that we wouldn't confuse Ray any worse than he was already confused, assuming he remembered me from my earlier visit. None of that mattered now. I sprinted across the lawn and realized that Shantel was right behind me. I turned and told her to wait outside before following Pete through the door.

Inside I heard Ray screaming at the top of his lungs in drunken English. "No!" was the only understandable sound coming from him.

Julio was firmly telling him to stop resisting arrest. As I crossed the living room, heading for the hallway where the struggle was taking place, Ray's screaming stopped. I came up behind Pete, who couldn't get in close enough to help Julio.

The hallway was dark, so dark that I could only just make out Julio kneeling over a shape on the floor. I knew from experience that Julio was snapping a set of cuffs on Ray. Julio recited Ray's rights and then tried to get him to stand up so he could lead him back out to the cruiser. But Ray wouldn't stand and Julio half dragged him back. Pete reached down and, as best he could in the cramped hall, grabbed one of Ray's shoulders and helped Julio drag him out into the living room. I backed up out of their way.

Once we had him in the light, I saw that there was blood on Ray's shirt, but it was Julio's nose that was bleeding.

"His elbow got me in the face."

Ray was struggling a bit. "Is he okay?" Pete asked.

"What?" Julio was trying to get his bleeding nose under control.

I looked down at Ray. "There's something wrong with him." I turned him over. His face was contorted and it had a blue tinge to it. "Uncuff him!" I yelled to Julio.

Julio dropped to the ground and took off the cuffs. We flipped Ray onto his back and I cleared his air passage, thinking he might be choking on his own vomit. But it was clear. Pete called for an ambulance over the radio.

We figured that Ray must have been having a heart attack. We had EMS on the radio giving us instructions. One of the worst aspects of living in a small town in a rural county is that the ambulance can be a long way off. Fifteen minutes was the estimated time of arrival. Julio had the most medical experience, so he began working on Ray while I went out to fetch his medical kit from the trunk of his cruiser.

I passed Shantel on my way to retrieve the medical bag. She was restraining herself from entering what was now a crime scene. Or, at the very least, an officer-involved incident scene.

Julio had been a corpsman in the military, so he was able to understand and follow the instructions that emergency services were giving to us over the radio. He'd also augmented his medical kit with more extensive supplies than most deputies carried. I was very glad that he was there to take the lead. As soon as a scene went medical, I turned a pale color of green. Not my thing.

By the time the ambulance arrived, Julio had a pulse, but little else. The EMS guys rushed Ray out of the house with Julio not far behind, leaving Pete and me inside the house staring at each other.

"What now?" Shantel asked from the front door.

"We need to get crime scene techs over here. If the suspect dies, there will have to be an investigation," Pete said. "Is Marcus on call?"

"I'll call him," Shantel said. It would still have to go

through the proper channels, but Shantel could get Marcus headed to the office to pick up the crime scene van.

At that moment, a thought struck me.

"Hey, let's check out the room in the back," I said to Pete, who was busy texting his wife that she should not wait up for him.

I found the switch for the light in the hall, but nothing happened. I turned on my flashlight and used it to navigate around some dirty laundry. The door to the bedroom was actually of a better quality than the one to the house. I tried the knob. The door was locked.

Damn it, the key could have been in Ray's pocket, I thought. "Pete, give me a hand."

Awkwardly crammed into the small hallway, we managed to get both of our shoulders against the door. I put my left foot against the far wall for leverage, then we did the count-of-three thing and pushed together. With a loud crack, the wood around the lock splintered and we stumbled into the dark room. The stench of human waste assaulted our noses. Pete found the light switch and turned it on.

My stomach dropped. Tonya was lying on a dirty old mattress, covered by a nasty-looking blanket. I rushed over and dropped down beside her. Relief flooded through me when I felt her warm face. I pulled the blanket back and saw that she was naked beneath it. I couldn't think about that right now.

I tried to wake her, but she didn't respond. "Call another ambulance!" I shouted to Pete, who was already on his radio and asking for assistance. I wanted to pick Tonya up and rush her to the hospital myself, but it would have been too risky to move her, not knowing what was wrong with her.

Pete was told it would be half an hour this time. Once we ascertained that her vital signs were steady, if weak, EMS advised us just to keep her warm and wait for the professionals.

"I need to get Shantel," I told Pete, who nodded solemnly.

Shantel was leaning against the door frame, talking on her phone. She hung up as soon as she saw me.

"We found her. She's stable, but I need you to remain as calm as you can. Tonya—" Shantel ran past me, not listening. I followed her and found her clutching Tonya, begging her to be all right.

It was well past one in the morning by the time we were all at the hospital and waiting for word from the doctors. Shantel was constantly on the phone with friends and relatives. I was glad she had something to do.

Julio had met us when we arrived and told us that the doctors didn't know whether Ray was going to survive or not. He'd had a series of heart attacks. They were running tests to determine how much damage had been done to his heart.

"He's a suspect in an abduction and kidnapping now. Possibly a sexual assault," Pete told Julio. We'd asked the doctors to perform a sexual assault exam once Tonya was stabilized. They assured us that they'd do what they could to preserve evidence, but their first priority was to save her life.

Nowhere does time move more slowly than in a hospital. After what seemed like an eternity, word came that they had stabilized Tonya, but that she'd sustained a massive blow to the back of her head and was in a coma. The doctors wanted to do an MRI and half a dozen other tests that had strange acronyms before they would feel confident that they completely understood her condition and could give a prognosis.

At three o'clock we finally received some good news. The doctors thought it was unlikely that Tonya had been sexually interfered with. I could see the relief on Shantel's face.

"Now we just have to pray for her to come back to us," Shantel said.

"Do you want me to drive you home?" I asked her.

"I can't go."

"You can't sleep in the ICU, and you won't get any rest in the waiting room. Why don't I take you to a motel?"

She smiled for the first time in hours. "I've got a place in the morgue," she said.

I had no idea what to say to that. My mind was too tired for riddles.

"A friend works downstairs and told me I can borrow the couch in her office."

"If you're sure."

She hugged me. "Thank you."

"I'm glad we found her."

CHAPTER EIGHT

My phone woke me up after a few hours' sleep. I didn't get it the first time, but it started ringing again almost immediately. "I Shot the Sheriff"—my new ringtone for Dad.

"Morning."

"It's almost noon."

"Almost."

"I heard you created a pile of work for us." His tone was flat. "You're quite the hero." His voice was still deadpan.

"Too early."

"I'm kidding. Not about the hero part. The *Democrat's* online headline says 'Deputy Rescues Kidnapped Girl.' They even spelled your name right. I can just hope that a few of the less educated voters get mixed up and think it was me."

He was obviously in a good mood. I could never decide whether he was easier to deal with when he was his normal grumpy self or when he was in a good mood. I think I preferred grumpy.

"The crime scene techs are out scouring Emery's place. Pete's in charge, obviously. And, unlike you, he didn't sleep in. I'll authorize the hours if you want to work on it too."

I took a minute to think about it. Was I going to get sucked back into the department? Maybe. But I really did want to work the case. "Yeah, I want to."

"Done," he said, hanging up.

I crawled out of bed, cleaned up quickly, fed Ivy even quicker and was back at ol' Ray's by one-thirty. Both of our crime scene vans were parked out front and Pete was napping in his car.

"Morning," I said, tapping on Pete's window. He'd apparently heard me walk up because he didn't move except to open one eye.

"You need better moccasins if you're going to sneak up on me."

"And if you're trying to hide, you need to figure out how to keep the windows from fogging up," I pointed out.

He rolled his window down. "I got up early. *After* you kept me out late on a very exciting date. Get in."

I had to move the flotsam and jetsam of a dozen carryout meals in order to find the passenger seat.

"They should be finishing up soon," Pete said, nodding at the house.

"Dad put me on the case."

"Must be nice to have friends in high places," he responded, sounding more like my old nemesis Matt Greene than like my old partner.

"Okay, we have got to clear the air."

"Clear away," he said soberly.

"You're pissed at me for resigning."

"Bingo."

"Why? This is not what I was meant to be. And I think last month proved it. I arrested a DEA agent and almost got my dad killed."

"Bullshit! You made a couple mistakes. Yes, we deal with high-risk situations and when we make a mistake, the consequences can be serious. Fine. But we're human and we're going to make mistakes. You just have to accept that. You're damned good at this," he said, waving his arms toward the vans. "As good as I am."

"No, I'm not. You *want* to be a deputy and you're good at

it. I don't want to be in a job where a mistake can cost someone their life."

He jabbed his finger at me. "Exactly. You're being a coward. Someone else is going to have your job, and that someone is going to be a human being, just like you, which means they're going to make mistakes, just like you would. You aren't stopping the mistakes from happening, you're just shielding yourself from criticism.

"You might remember that I once made a mistake that almost cost Matt his life. I was stuffing my fat face while a fellow officer was being shot at not half a mile away. A report was made, a reprimand was given. And you know what I did? I sucked it up and took the humiliation. I could have run off to some other county or police department. I had to work with Matt for years, taking all his insults and nasty looks. And you know what the worst part of it was? In my heart, I knew his anger was justified." He stopped, breathless from his tirade.

"So I'm a coward. What's that to you?"

"You're my friend. If someone is going to make a mistake and possibly get me killed, I want it to be a friend." Pete mumbled the last part, as though embarrassed to admit it.

His words stung a bit, but I was glad we were finally talking about it. "I'm sorry that I didn't talk to you before I resigned. What do they say in AA? One day at a time? For now, for this case, let's just pretend that everything is back to normal," I said, putting out my hand. After a moment, Pete took it and shook.

"I guess I can do that," Pete said, looking out his window. "So what the heck do you think went on in there?"

"I don't know," I said honestly. I told him about Ray groping Tonya at the Sweet Spot.

"Sexually assaulting," he corrected me.

"Right. By the bartender's account, she left first. Ray might have found her outside when he left and... what? Lured her back to his house? That seems unlikely after what went on inside the bar. Honestly, I think he would've had a hard time luring her even if he hadn't just assaulted her. He's not a very charming individual."

"So he hit her and then dragged her back to his house? Sober, he'd have a hard time doing that. Drunk, it's even less likely. And he hasn't been sober in decades," Pete speculated.

"Maybe she was walking past his house, needed help with something and decided to knock on the door?"

"Possibly, but you said she left before him. And we found her phone in Ray's house, and it's working. If she needed help, she could have called one of her friends."

"Yeah, Jarvis would walk across molten glass to help that girl," I said.

"What aren't we seeing?" Pete asked.

"Why was Ray keeping her locked up?"

"Maybe he just liked to look at her. Weirdos do weird things, that's why we call them weirdos," Pete said.

"Thank you for that deep insight into deviant sexual behavior," I said, enjoying being on good terms with Pete again.

"Maybe we'll just have to wait until one or both of them are conscious."

"Even when they wake up, it's going to be iffy whether we get the real story. He'll probably lie to us and, with Tonya's head injuries, she's unlikely to recall the time around the incident," I despaired.

"I'm going to ask Dr. Darzi to look at her head wound. Maybe he can give us some idea of what caused it."

"Good idea. Damn. I just realized that we need to do a search of the area between the Sweet Spot and Ray's house for evidence."

"Should have thought of that." Pete opened his door and lifted his bulk out.

I was close behind him. We made a quick stop at the house to let the techs know we'd be adding to their workload. Marcus was there and asked about Tonya and

Shantel. His wife, Esther, Shantel's best friend, had gone to the hospital that morning, but he hadn't heard anything from her. We told him what little we knew, then he went back to dusting for prints, looking lost without Shantel beside him.

Pete and I started walking from the house to the Sweet Spot, trying to decide how large an area the techs should cover when they finished with the house. We kept our eyes open as we walked, hoping for the once-in-a-blue-moon chance of finding a piece of obvious evidence.

"There wasn't much blood," Pete said to himself as much as to me.

"Maybe he used a piece of concrete or a stick."

The neighborhood was poor and there was a lot of trash along the street. Bottles and cigarette packages, mostly, effluvium from the Sweet Spot's customers. There was also a disturbing amount of condom wrappers, used condoms and the small plastic jewelry bags, about an inch square, used to distribute drugs. It would make anyone shudder to think what went on in this neighborhood.

"Hard to believe that we can be walking through this crap and look up and see yards with children's toys," I said, voicing my frustration.

"It's not like we haven't tried shutting the place down," Pete said as his eyes scanned the ground, looking for anything that might have been related to Tonya's assault.

I was grateful for the weather, dry with a clear blue sky and cool air. Luckily it hadn't rained since Tonya disappeared, so if we *could* find a weapon, there was a good chance there would still be DNA on it.

We found a few items, but nothing that was clearly related to Tonya. We marked the area off with crime scene tape until the techs could take another look. Then I headed to the hospital in Tallahassee. The thirty-five-minute drive gave me an opportunity to try and make sense of everything, but by the time I arrived I still had nothing.

I found Shantel in the ICU waiting area with other friends and family, including Jarvis. I took her down to the cafeteria for coffee and finally told her about Ray's public groping of Tonya. She cried some more.

"I just feel like I've let her down since she finished high school. I thought maybe I'd watched over her too close when she was a teenager. When she graduated, I thought she'd made it. Wouldn't need me as much."

"You can't regret the past."

Shantel looked up and gave me a little smile. "Look who's talking."

"You know I did that on purpose." I smiled back.

"I got to pray. I know that. I can't let my own self-pity cloud my judgment. I've got to get my head on straight and see Tonya through this. The doctor says that she's going to be in a coma for a few more days, maybe longer. They think she'd come out of it if they let her, but they want to keep her there until the swelling in her head goes down. Doctors talk a lot. I think that's to keep you from realizing how little they know."

"At least it wasn't the Hacker," I said, remembering Shantel's earlier anxiety. She looked up at me.

"Funny, I'd already forgotten about that. And yesterday it was my biggest fear."

"Did the report you saw actually mention the Hacker?"

"By name. It listed a dozen points of comparison and at least four were ones that hadn't been made public," Shantel said.

I thought that talking about the Hacker would be a good way to distract Shantel, even just for a few minutes.

"They only had the one case, right? When was the body found?"

"Almost a month ago. Near the county line."

"Was she from Adams County?"

"Yeah, north side near the trailer park."

"Where Tonya's friend Jenny's boyfriend lives."

"And where Tonya was last known to be. Until you traced her to the Sweet Spot."

"That idiot Jenny could have saved us some time there. It

felt like forever before she mentioned that important detail."

"In her airhead way, she thought she was helping Tonya. When I was Tonya's age, I'd have been royally pissed at any friend of mine that ratted me out to my family." Shantel gave a little laugh. "Jenny *did* call and ask about Tonya. She almost apologized."

"Funny thing is, I can't stop thinking about the Hacker. What's Dad going to do if he *is* back?"

"Could he really be back? I mean, after all this time?"

"Wouldn't be the first time that a serial killer went dormant only to come back and kill again. There are people who think that the Zodiac Killer and the Unabomber are one in the same. A psychopath can fool you. They can learn to mimic human emotion. Blend in. The BTK Killer stopped for fourteen years."

"Now you're just giving me the creeps." She shuddered.

"We can hope that the Leon County Sheriff's Office is over-reacting. I just wish I could warn my dad. All the trouble between us came from me holding information back from him, and now I'm doing it again."

"I'd say I'm sorry for dragging you into this, but the fact is, I'm glad. I told you, our department needs you. You're a great investigator."

I waived my hand dismissively. "Pete would have already been on top of it if they weren't short-handed. Speaking of which, Pete's asked Dr. Darzi to look at Tonya's wounds from a forensic perspective." I wanted to give Shantel a heads-up about that.

"You think he can help pin this on that drunken monster?"

"Pete thought he might give us some insight into what weapon we're looking for and what type of attack she was subjected to."

"Pete's good, but you and Pete together are better. Just think about it," she said, standing up. "I've got to get back up to the ICU."

"Let me know how Tonya's doing."

"I will. You keep me up on the investigation."

I gave her a thumbs up and, on that note, decided I'd better check in on our suspect. I went back upstairs to the cardiac wing, where it took me the better part of an hour to find someone who knew something.

"It isn't unusual for a patient who's suffered a severe cardiac event to go into a coma. This patient has a number of risk factors that make his recovery problematic," the doctor explained.

"What's the bottom line?"

"I doubt he'll regain consciousness in less than a couple of days. And any neurologic prognosis that I give you in the first seventy-two hours is going to be unreliable. There's your bottom line. Come back in a couple of days," he said and walked away.

I called Pete and gave him an update.

"I've officially released Ray Emery from custody," he told me.

"What?" I asked, louder than I intended.

"Just until we see how his medical situation shakes out. Your dad told me to do it. It's not like Ray's going to hop a plane for South America. And your dad said the department couldn't afford to be liable for his hospital bills," Pete explained. "And I've tracked down the bartender from the Sweet Spot. We're going to pick him up for questioning, if you want to meet us back at the office."

"Roger that." I was looking forward to talking with the bartender when I had the home court advantage.

CHAPTER NINE

I got to the office before Pete and the bartender. It was awkward not having a desk to go to and not really wanting to talk to anyone, though Dill Kirby, the old desk sergeant, did congratulate me on finding Tonya and thwarting a kidnapping.

While I was pacing around the hall in front of the interview room, a woman walked in. She looked familiar. She was well dressed and carried a small notebook. She smiled at me and I realized who it was—Officer Darlene Marks of the Calhoun Police Department.

"Officer Marks. What are you doing here?"

"Ex-deputy Macklin, I could ask you the same question. Rumor has it you quit," she kidded me.

"The news of my resignation has been somewhat exaggerated. I'm still a reserve deputy. Actually, I'm waiting to interview a witness. What about you?" I wasn't going to let her get away with changing the subject.

"I'm here for an interview too. For your job. Or maybe Matt's," she answered, smiling at my reaction.

"Pete mentioned they might hire an investigator from outside the department. That's a surprise."

"I guess with so many of you quitting, being killed or

getting arrested all in the same month, the sheriff had to look outside the department," Darl, as she liked to be called, shot back. It was all good-natured banter, though there was a slight edge to it. Darl had a way of getting under my skin.

"Good luck."

"It's not about luck." She winked at me and headed for my father's office. A couple minutes later I heard a huge bark come from that direction. Dad loved to have Mauser, his two-year-old, one-hundred-and-ninety-pound Great Dane, sit in on interviews. The rumor around the station was that Mauser actually approved all hires and promotions. After an interview, everyone always asked if you got a paws up or a paws down.

Pete showed up a few minutes later with a very unhappy-looking bartender in tow.

"I knew you were trouble," he said to me before we even sat down.

Pete introduced him. "This is one Thomas Jackson, AKA Topman, twenty-eight-years old and an employee of the Sweet Spot for the past eight months. He has several convictions on his record, though so far just misdemeanors for possession. Mr. Jackson, you realize that if you get a felony you won't be able to be a bartender?"

"It's not like it's my career or anything," he said, looking down at the table.

"No, I would imagine your actual career involves breaking the law on a regular basis. We may get back to that. Right now we're interested in events that took place at the Sweet Spot on Saturday night."

"I don't know anything about it."

"First of all, we didn't tell you what event and, second, you've already let on that you saw this sexual assault take place," I told him.

His head jerked up. "I don't know about any sexual assault. What the hell are you talking about?"

"You told me that you saw ol' Ray grope Tonya Williams at the Sweet Spot on Saturday night."

"Hell, he grabbed her tits and maybe a little ass, but he didn't rape her or nothin'," Jackson said, shaking his head.

"I'm going to tell you something that might save you some time in jail later in life. Grabbing someone's private parts is sexual assault."

"Since when?" he asked, sounding genuinely surprised to learn this.

"Just believe me and remember it. Saturday night, you're tending bar at your gentleman's club and Tonya came in. Did anyone else besides Ray pay any attention to her?"

"No, I told you, the tw… girl came in and I sent her away."

"Which reminds me. You also forgot to mention that she'd been in there before with Jarvis Monroe, whose uncle is a regular."

Jackson's eyes went back to the table. "So? You didn't ask."

"And we aren't going to play those games this time. You tell me everything, and I mean everything, you think I might be interested in. Now, to save time, I'll tell you right now that I have no interest in anything like drugs or prostitution if it does not relate directly to Tonya Williams. So you don't have to worry that you'll get in trouble with your boss. Unless," I hit the table with my fist, wanting to make an impression, "unless you fail to tell me everything that relates to Tonya. If I find out that you left anything out or lied, I *will* find a way to screw you. If that means making it look like you're cooperating with the current prosecution of the Thompsons, I'll do that." He looked a bit frightened by this. "I guess you can imagine what they would do to someone they thought was testifying against them."

"Just ask your damn questions. Yes, she came in. Yes, she'd been in before with that candy-ass, so what? Saturday she was by herself. Like I told you, when she was leaving, Ray grabbed her. The place was crowded so I couldn't see real well, but I saw him reach for her tit… breasts and maybe her butt. She screams like she hasn't ever been touched before and hits out at ol' Ray, who almost falls over. The old wino was already stumbling drunk. I was afraid I was going to have to roll him out the door. I've had to do that. Roll him out the door when we were closing. Do you believe that shit?"

"How drunk was he at the time he grabbed Tonya? Unstable drunk? Could she have fought him off if he'd persisted?"

"My five-year-old son could have knocked that old drunk over. Like I said, I was afraid he'd be a pain in my ass later, so I was watching him. That's how I know he left about ten minutes after that girl."

"Ten minutes. Could it have been five minutes? Or fifteen?" I pressed him.

"Not fifteen. Sooner, maybe closer to five. When I saw him leave not long after her, I thought there goes two problems out the door."

"He didn't come back?"

Jackson shook his head. "Funny about that, he hasn't been back since."

"That's unusual?"

"You kidding? Some days he's in there as soon as I open the door. The old fool just lives up the street."

"Later, did anyone mention something happening outside?"

"Yeah, some guys were laughing about some fool who got hauled off for pissing at a cop. Nothing else."

"One last chance. Did anything else odd happen that night? Think hard."

Surprisingly, he looked like he was thinking about it. "No. Nothing."

"What time did you close up?"

"I locked the door at two. I was home by three."

"When you left, did you see anything or anyone outside the building?"

"Funny you say that. Now I remember there *was* a car there. I kinda looked in it to see if any of the girls were making money there." He seemed to realize what he'd said and looked up at me with a chagrined expression.

"Don't worry, I meant it when I said we weren't interested in prostitution today. What type of car was it?"

"I don't know. A piece of crap like most of the cars at the Sweet Spot."

"Color?"

"I don't know. It was late," he whined.

"Was the car light or dark?"

"Dark. Maybe blue."

"Was it there the next morning?"

"Nope, gone."

I exchanged a glance with Pete. Based on the description that Shantel had given us, this certainly could have been Tonya's car. But where was it now?

"What time did you get there on Sunday?"

"Noon. Time to clean up a bit. We can't serve liquor on Sunday until one o'clock."

"Anything else?" I asked Pete, who shook his head.

We had Jackson write up a witness statement and sign it. It turned out to be surprisingly articulate. As we were escorting him out the door, he turned and told me he hoped that we locked the drunk bastard up for good. When I told him that the old man was probably going to die, Jackson got an odd expression on his face and said he hoped he'd be okay. Human beings are very odd creatures.

My watch said it was quitting time. I realized I was going to have to keep track of all my hours for this since I wasn't a full-time investigator. What a pain.

I invited Cara over for dinner. An evening in her company more than made up for the frustrations of the previous two days.

CHAPTER TEN

Thursday morning, they operated on Tonya to relieve pressure on her brain. Medical stuff eeks me out, so I didn't concentrate on the details. What was important was that she came through the operation well, and the doctors had high hopes for her recovery. What they didn't have high hopes for was her memory of the events surrounding the attack.

Pete called me that afternoon and put me on a conference call with Dr. Darzi, who'd finally had a chance to examine Tonya. "She took a very hard blow to the back of the head. The object used was rounded. A lead pipe or a baseball bat would fit the profile."

"Could you tell how tall the man was?" Pete asked.

"If it was a man. Using a pipe or bat, this wound could have been inflicted by a woman. How tall... The victim is 5'6". The shoes she was wearing were described to me as having very little heal. The attacker would have been taller than her, maybe 5'10" to six foot. And the blow came from behind, right to left. That indicates a right-handed attacker."

I wondered how tall Ray was. Shorter than 5'10", I thought, but maybe that was just because I'd only seen him drunk and stooped over.

"Was it only one blow?" I asked.

"Yes. One."

We thanked him and he hung up. "What do you think?" Pete asked me.

"I don't know. I doubt our drunk would have been able to deliver one solid blow. I would expect hesitation. The man's not known for being violent."

"And he'd have to stand up straight to come close to 5'10". So are we looking for another assailant?"

"That's what I'm thinking. We'll need to find out who else was in that parking lot. And how did she end up at Ray's? Did she stumble there after being clubbed?"

"Who the hell knows? Hey, guess who your dad interviewed for your old job?"

"I saw her when she came in for the interview."

"Did she pull her gun on you?"

"Ha, ha. Everyone loves you for your sense of humor."

"I know. Why don't you follow up at the Sweet Spot and see if you can get a few names of patrons that might have been hanging out in the parking lot."

"I've got one already. The pisser that Julio picked up."

"Hey, that's right. Follow up on that." Pete was enjoying his role as the lead investigator.

"Thanks."

"Since you quit, I'm juggling about ten cases from assault and battery to murder and you have one. I don't want to hear your whining."

We bantered back and forth for a few more minutes before I called Julio and arranged to meet him at the Sweet Spot. He regularly patrolled the area so he could give me info on all the regulars.

Julio and I drove by every wannabe crack house in the Sweetgum neighborhood, looking for the Sweet Spot regulars. Actually, most of those folks never even entered the bar, they just conducted business in the parking lot. It left me feeling like I should gather up the honest people stuck in the neighborhood and take them someplace safe.

The neighborhood had a few older people who had

bought their homes when it was one of the only subdivisions that people of color could move into. Younger people were moving in now, because it was the only area they could afford, and they were striving to make it better. These two groups had been petitioning the county commission for years to condemn the Sweet Spot and to enforce county codes covering yards and homes. But the Thompsons, who not only owned the Sweet Spot but also a dozen homes in the area, had attorneys that knew all the tricks. That, combined with the efforts of a few other slum lords, ensured that anyone trying to change things would find it a Sisyphean task.

Predictably, no one we talked to had seen anything. The only one who admitted seeing Tonya was Julio's pisser, Tyrone Lamont, who claimed that's why he was turned toward the street. He said he saw her and turned away out of embarrassment.

"You aren't just telling us this because you think it might excuse your public urination, are you?" I questioned him.

Tyrone's soft, intelligent eyes seemed to be at odds with the behavior he was accused of.

"No. Look, I'd just got paid for a big job I did. My AC company did the install for a new building in an industrial park in Tallahassee. I was just cutting the fool."

"And you couldn't find a better place to do it at?" I was incredulous.

"No, man, don't do me like that. I was with an old buddy of mine. He's been down on his luck. I thought we could go out and celebrate my good luck. Guy's a mess. I made the mistake of taking him on to work with me for a while, but he couldn't handle it."

"But you definitely saw her?" I showed him Tonya's picture again.

"I'm pretty sure. It was dark, I was drunk. But, yeah, she was wearing a sparkly silver dress. Something like that." This jived with what we knew. Tonya had been wearing a silver dress with sequins running from the waist down.

"What was she doing when you saw her?"

"Walking away from the bar. I think toward the parking lot."

The only other help Tyrone could offer was to contact his friend. He had to be very persuasive to get his buddy to talk to us. In turn, we agreed to take care of the public urination charge.

We met Rog, as he preferred to be called, at the Express Burgers where we bought him a bargain meal with the promise of a milkshake if he cooperated.

"Yeah, I saw her. I was too busy getting… You don't care about nothing else but the girl?"

"Pinkie swear," I told him.

"Tyrone says I can talk to you. Okay, I was starting to get pretty high by the time I saw her. Wasn't looking for skirt. 'Sides, she was too skinny for me. She looked upset and was headed for the cars. That's all."

"You were near the door of the bar?"

"Buying… Uh, yeah. There were a couple of us. Don't even ask for their names, man, they'd beat the crap out of me. They're some mean bastards, but you got to go where the flow is."

"Did you see an old man come out of the bar?"

"Old man? What do I care about an old man?"

"He was pretty drunk."

"Oh, yeah, Xmax slugged him pretty good." Rog made boxing motions with his hands and then quickly went back to eating his fries.

"Xmax?"

"No, no. I didn't say no names. No. That old dude come out and he stumbled into… someone. The, uhh, someone punched the old man in the shoulder."

"What'd the old man do?"

Rog laughed and shook his head. "What do you think he did? He fell down."

"All the way to the ground?"

"No, just down to his knees. Didn't even look at… the

guy who hit him. Just crawled a couple feet on his hands and knees then got up, walked off. Funny as shit."

Even the offer of the milkshake couldn't pry any more useful information from Rog.

I called it a day and headed home to feed Ivy before joining Cara at her place for dinner. As I was leaving I got a text from Dad: *How are you coming on Tonya's case?*

I texted back: *Getting there*, being intentionally vague. I was carefully avoiding seeing Dad in person. Having to keep Shantel's secret about the file she saw, I didn't want to be face-to-face with Dad right now. Part of the reason I'd felt so bad about the events of last month, and why I had quit, was because I had kept him in the dark for so long. This time, if I said anything I would be betraying a friend. But by not talking I was betraying my father. *How do I get myself into these situations?* I wondered.

Cara was waiting with a pizza when I got to her place. Alvin was all about the pizza and the only way we could get some peace from the wrinkle-faced Pug was to give him a Kong filled with peanut butter.

"He can't have pizza. The little guy's digestion isn't good on the best of days," Cara told me.

"I'm laughing over the Kong. Dad has one about the size of Alvin for Mauser."

Mauser was probably the most spoiled Great Dane in the world and, from some pictures I've seen on Facebook, that's saying something. Dad had become even more indulgent with him since last month's parade. Dad insisted that Mauser was facing down Mark Edwards while the corrupt deputy held a gun on him. I've pointed out that anytime Dad lay on the floor, Mauser seemed to have an uncontrollable urge to come and sit on him. But my arguments were ignored. Even though I was the one who rode a horse straight at the killer, it was Mauser who got all the credit. And, yes, I was jealous of my long-tailed brother.

CHAPTER ELEVEN

I'd planned to spend most of Friday researching careers that I might be qualified for. Law enforcement can open up some interesting doors, but for some opportunities I would need more education. I'd always enjoyed school, but the thought of it now seemed a bit like going backward.

My plans didn't matter. I got a call from Pete at ten o'clock. Ray was regaining consciousness, but the doctors didn't know how long it would be before he lapsed back into a coma or suffered any number of possible catastrophic medical events.

When I got to the hospital, Pete was sitting outside on a bench waiting for me. "I really hate hospitals," he told me, finishing a text and putting his phone away.

"All sane people hate hospitals," I said as we walked inside.

Upstairs we had to once again hunt for someone who could advise us on Ray's condition. Eventually we found the doctor in charge.

"Mr. Emery's condition is not good. He's awake now, but I've seen this before. His body is rallying, but I'm afraid the battle has already been decided."

"Have you all been able to locate any relatives?" I asked.

"I had one of our interns work on it all day yesterday. I even sent her to his house. We're pretty sure that he doesn't have any family. He apparently lived in Atlanta for a while before moving here to be with his wife's family, but they split up decades ago and what's left of his wife's family doesn't want anything to do with him. And none of them ever heard him talk about any relatives."

"Can we talk to him?" Pete asked the million-dollar question.

"I could not let you in, in which case this man will have no one with a connection to his outside life to talk to during what will probably be his last lucid moments. Or I could let you talk with him, and take the chance that you might upset him and possibly worsen his condition." The doctor paused. "I'm a live-life-to-the-fullest kind of guy. If I was him, I'd want to talk with you no matter what news you brought. But I caution you. Don't over-excite him or your interview will be over. Do you understand?"

"Of course," Pete answered.

The doctor introduced us to a burly male nurse who looked more like a bouncer. The mountain led us into the ICU and to Ray's bed.

It was difficult to look at him. Entwined in tubes, he lay there shrunken and alone.

"Water," he croaked. The nurse stepped forward and offered him water through a straw, drawing it back before the old man was finished.

"Can't overdo it now, Mr. Emery."

Ray growled at him, "I'm dying and I'm sober. What the hell?"

"Ray, I'm Deputy Pete Henley from the sheriff's office."

"You attacked me! Where's the girl?" His eyes darted about as though he expected to see Tonya standing in the corner of the room.

"That's why we're here, Mr. Emery. Why did you assault the girl?" I asked.

Ray's eyes went wide and he looked crazed. "I didn't do

nothing to her. It was him."

"Who?"

"A man I don't know…" He started to wheeze and couldn't catch his breath. I was afraid the nurse was going to call a halt to the session, but he waited and Ray's coughing subsided. He started again, "In the dark, by her car. He hit her."

"So you're claiming that another man hit her."

"I ain't claiming. You bastards. I knew you'd think I did it. I helped her. But I knew you'd come for me." He sounded bitter and resigned.

"Mr. Emery, we know that you assaulted Tonya inside the bar," I said.

He stared at me. "I did no such thing. Liar!" he sputtered.

"We have a witness who says you put your hand on her breasts and buttocks."

"Hell, yeah, I did that, but I didn't assault her. Just having fun."

"That is assault. It's sexual assault to touch someone's body without permission."

Ray snorted. "I never forced myself on no woman. A little touchy-feely, ain't no harm in it. The world's gone crazy."

"You will have to take my word for it. What you did was a criminal act."

"The joke's on you. You bastards have killed me. You won't be putting me in prison," he said defiantly. He had us there. Then his eyes grew soft. "How's the girl?"

"Alive, no thanks to you," Pete told him.

"I didn't know what to do. When I came up behind them, I seen the man go to swing this stubby bat, and I yelled as best I could. But I was too late. He hit her and turned on me. I thought he would kill me, but he just looked startled. He ran off."

"Which way did he run?"

"Away from the bar through the vacant lot. I tried to help her. She could stand. Sort of. I told her she could come to my place and sit down. I don't think she knew where she was. I took her and led her over to my house."

I thought about how close Julio had been to stepping in when he saw Tonya in the yard. Ray must have been on the other side of her.

"When we got to my place, she sat down on the couch and then just fell over. There weren't a lot of blood so I thought after she rested she'd be fine. But she never woke up. Still lying on my couch in the morning. I tried to clean her up, but her clothes were a mess."

"You took her clothes off?" Pete asked.

"Yeah, but I didn't touch nothin'. It wouldn't have been right, with her sick like that."

I believed him. "So why didn't you call 911?"

"You all would have come in and beat me. I was more sober in the morning. Scared. I figured if she woke up on her own, I could explain things. She'd see that I'd helped her."

Unlikely, I thought. "So what did you do?"

"I made up a bed in my back room. I was as careful as I could be getting her back there. I slid her on a blanket. Once I got her there, I did everything I could to make her comfortable. I tried to get her to drink some water, but she was gone. I started getting even more scared, thinking about someone coming to look for her. Then I remembered her car, so I went back up there and moved it."

"Where is the car?"

"A metal shed near my house. I got the key. The guy who owns it lives up north, so I watch it for him," Ray said. *Who lets a drunk watch anything for him?* I wondered. Of course, that wasn't much of a riddle as the answer came to me almost instantly: *Another drunk.*

Ray went into another coughing fit. I held my breath. I wanted just a little more time with him. What could he tell us about the man who'd hit Tonya?

After he'd been given a little more water, Ray looked at Pete and me with eyes that wanted... what? Absolution? His breathing had become very labored.

"I can't let you stay much longer," the nurse said.

"Just a couple more questions," I told him. Turning to Ray, I said, "You can still do something for Tonya. Help us find the man that did this."

"She was so pretty," he said, his eyes taking on a glassy look.

"Please, Ray, what kind of clothes was he wearing?"

"The son of a bitch was pretty tall," Ray said. "Wearing? I don't know. A coat. Dark."

"Was the coat dark or are you talking about the light?"

"The coat was dark."

"His face. You said he turned around. What did his face look like?"

"Funny," Ray said dreamily.

"Funny how?"

"White, it was very white, and his eyes were sunken in like… Odd. I don't know. Gloves, he had gloves on."

"What kind?"

"Just gloves. Maybe work gloves."

Ray's wheezing turned to full-blown gasps. His arms started jerking around and the nurse ordered us out as he drew a syringe of something and administered it to Ray's IV.

Pete and I left the ICU. "You believe him?" Pete asked.

"I do. He may be a drunk, but I think he was being honest. Oddly, he did save Tonya's life."

"Of course, he almost killed her by not calling 911."

"I think his impending death is going to resolve that moral dilemma for us," I said.

"What about this mystery man?"

"I think we need to put everything we've got into finding him." I had a sinking feeling about that mystery man and there was only one person I could talk to about it. "I'm going to go find Shantel and tell her what Ray told us. I'll meet you out front."

I found Shantel sitting with Tonya. She came out when she saw me. "Tonya's doing better, but the doctors think it might be a couple more days before she wakes up," Shantel told me, anxiety on her face and hope in her eyes.

"We talked with Ray Emery. He's dying." I told her everything he'd told us.

"But…" She was speechless.

"We're in a bind here. You found out something that you shouldn't have. And because of that knowledge, we might have a very important lead on a serial killer."

"I'll go to the Leon County Sheriff's Office and tell them. I've got to make sure that my friend is protected."

"Actually, there's a way that we can get around this without anyone falling on their swords. You'll have to admit to your friend that you were snooping, but when you give him this lead and connect up his case with a potential witness, I think he'll forgive you. Besides, anyone who knows you would expect you to snoop if you're left unattended around a pile of case files." I smiled at her.

"Thank you. That makes me feel better. I'll call him now. I don't want to be accused of sitting on this information," Shantel said as she pulled her phone out of her jacket pocket.

"What I need from them is permission to tell Pete and my dad," I said soberly.

"I understand." She dialed and waited for an answer. "Hey, what's up? I've got a confession to make." She explained what she'd done and what had happened to Tonya, but then she got a funny expression on her face as she listened to the voice on the other line.

At the same time, my phone rang. When I answered, Pete told me a body had just been discovered in the woods by the county line. Shantel was still talking to her friend, but I could tell that they were having the same conversation.

"I'm going there now," I told her, running out the door.

CHAPTER TWELVE

By the time I got to the scene, half a dozen deputies from Leon County and Adams County were talking and shaking their heads on the outside of a streamer of crime scene tape stretching across the dirt road. As I got out of my car, I could see Pete's large frame about fifty yards on the other side of the tape. He was talking to another suit, presumably the detective from the Leon County Sheriff's Office who was leading their investigation.

The dirt road was raised and ran through a thousand acres of swamp that straddled the two counties. Here and there were areas high enough to hunt or grow pine trees, but most of it was swamp made up of cypress, sweetgum, magnolia and red maple.

I heard a vehicle coming down the road behind me and turned to see Dad's truck, a plume of dust being thrown up behind it. He was out of the truck before the dust settled.

"Have you seen the body?" was his greeting to me.

"No, I just got here."

"At least they're keeping everyone back," he said, though I knew he wanted nothing more than to walk down that road to take a look at the crime scene.

Dad looked around. "How close are we to the county

line? Can't be far."

"Out here it's hard to tell exactly where it is," answered one of the Leon County deputies.

"Do you think it's him?" I asked Dad, sure he'd know exactly who I meant.

"I hate to admit it, but I hope so. I want another chance to catch the bastard. I just found out that Leon County found a body a few weeks ago that might be related," he told me.

My heart pounded in my chest. I wanted to tell him that I already knew, just to have my deception out on the table, but sometimes discretion is the better part of valor. "I'll be interested to see the file," was all I said.

Pete was heading our way. He walked very carefully along a designated track so that he didn't disturb any evidence.

"The crime scene techs are going to film everything and cast the footprints and tire tracks, then they'll let everyone come in. Tolland said you can come take a look now if you want." Pete directed this last comment to Dad.

"No, I'll wait." Dad hated to look like he had special privileges. He'd spent many years as a deputy and never considered himself better than anyone else.

Leon County's crime scene techs had shown up first since their investigators had arrived before ours, and no one was exactly sure whose jurisdiction it was. But Dad had still called one of our teams out. Marcus pulled up in the crime scene van as we waited and watched the Leon County techs log and film everything.

"What do you want me to do?" Marcus asked.

"Right now, just watch," Dad said.

Investigator Cedrick Tolland walked over to us. Tolland had been with the Leon County Sheriff's Office for almost as long as Dad had been with Adams County. Tolland was tall and grizzled-looking. If you squinted you could see a slight resemblance to Clint Eastwood, which had earned him the nickname Dirty Harry. This was particularly funny since

A. E. HOWE

Tolland was known as one of the most easygoing guys in the department, always helping out stray dogs and the homeless. Some said he was a bit too easygoing with girlfriends and ex-wives that took unfair advantage of him. But he was also respected as one of the smartest and most successful investigators in Florida.

"Ted." Tolland nodded to my father. "Rick." Dad nodded back. They were the picture of two Old West lawmen with their laconic greetings and stoic expressions.

"How's your boy doing?" Tolland asked Dad as though I wasn't standing five feet away.

"You know kids," was Dad's answer.

"Trouble."

"You got it." They both glanced over at me with slight smiles on their faces, but their gazes quickly returned to the men and women working on the other side of the crime scene tape.

"Is it him?" Dad asked.

"I'd bet money on it," Tolland responded.

"Who's got jurisdiction on this one?" Dad asked.

"We'd have to get a surveyor in to know for sure. I say you take it. We got the first one."

"We should form a joint task force and include the cold cases," Dad said.

"We're going to catch him this time."

"Damn straight."

I waved Pete over to a spot far enough away from everyone else that we wouldn't be overheard.

"I think there is a chance that Tonya's assault is connected," I told him.

Pete thought about this. "It's possible. But we shouldn't jump to conclusions."

"You're right, we have to keep an open mind. But I'm pretty confident that Ray was telling the truth."

"I agree about Ray. Now as to whether Tonya's case is related to the Hacker... I see some of the similarities. Tonya was clubbed on the back of the head. All of the Hacker victims were taken, as far as we know, from Adams County. Most were in lower income neighborhoods or seedy parts of town. Have I missed anything else?"

"So far that's all. But I'm thinking that if this victim was taken the same night, or even the next night after Tonya's assault, that would be quite a coincidence."

Pete nodded. "Tonya was his first choice, but Kay spooked him so he abandoned Tonya and found whoever this poor girl is. I can see that."

"I think we need to tell Dad and Tolland about our suspicions."

"Makes sense," Pete agreed and we walked back over to the two crusty old lawmen.

When we finished telling them about Tonya, they both looked thoughtful. After a minute, Dad turned to Pete. "I want you to arrange a protection detail for Tonya."

"We can help with that. After all, she's in a Tallahassee hospital. If we have a live witness, we've got to keep her alive," Tolland said.

"I think the old man saw more than she did, but the doctors don't give him long," I said.

"See if you can get the hospital to put them in the same ICU ward so we can protect both of them. And have someone notify us immediately if he regains consciousness. Maybe we'll get lucky," Dad said.

"Pete and I are going to scour the neighborhood behind the parking lot. He went in that direction. Probably doesn't live there, so maybe someone saw him or his vehicle," I told them.

"Last time around we assumed he drove a pickup. We got a couple casts from tires, but could never be sure if they were from his vehicle. Like this." Tolland waved at the sandy road that had just enough clay in it to turn it orange. We hadn't had rain in several days, and every time the wind blew, dust rose up off the road. "The roads were sandy and too many other vehicles had passed over them. Same here. There are a couple of houses out in the woods at the end of the road, so there's been a fair amount of traffic."

As if on cue, one of Leon County's crime scene techs came over to Tolland and told him that they'd gotten everything they could off of the road.

Ten minutes later, a group of us was standing on the raised road, looking down at the body of a young white woman, partly hidden on a small elevated piece of ground surrounded by swampy water. She was lying face down, and I could see a series of hacks in her back.

There was a cruelty to these murders that made them especially hard to stomach. Serial killers murder for pleasure or out of some deep-seated violent impulse. What was the motive for the Zodiac murders? People always speculated, but no one knew. The Boston Strangler killed because of the neighbor's dog? Who really knew? Serial killers are simply broken. Defective. What's most frightening about them is that they can blend in and fool us into believing that they're just like us.

Two forensic techs were with the body, taking pictures, body temperature, and going over the clothes with sticky tape to collect any evidence on her backside before they turned her over. No one had even seen her face yet. The killer didn't remove any of the victims' clothes, and he'd always left wallets and identification. Sex and profit didn't seem to interest him.

I saw one of the techs reach into the victim's coat pocket and remove a small coin purse. He opened it and took out a driver's license.

"Dawn Hall," he read. "She was twenty-two years old." I thought that was all he was going to say, but then he added in a sad tone, "Her birthday is in two weeks." The young tech put the license in an evidence bag before walking carefully through the mud and over to the road. Tolland reached down and took the bagged card.

"Like the rest of the victims, she's from Adams County." He handed the bag to Dad.

He looked at it and then turned to Pete and me. "You all

may be onto something. Her address is near the Sweet Spot. It's going to be interesting to see what kind of time frame Dr. Datzi gives us."

"Why did you think he used a pickup truck for the earlier murders?" Pete asked. If we had a lead on the type of vehicle he used, it might be useful when we canvassed the area around the Sweet Spot and the victim's home.

"We never found any fibers like the type you'd expect from the carpet and upholstery in a car."

"Could have been a utility van," Pete said.

"We thought about that, but the fact that he chose dirt roads in the back country to access his dump sites made a pickup truck more likely. Probably he just put the body in the bed of the truck and covered it up with a tarp or something," Dad said.

"The sad thing is, we would have gotten further if he'd left DNA, but all he does is club them and then hack at them with a cleaver. Most likely he wears gloves. Maybe that's why he's only killed during the cooler months. So he can wear more clothes without being too suspicious," Tolland added.

"Or sweating on the victims," Pete said.

"Can we get a look at the old files?" I asked.

Dad gave me a look and I knew he wanted to make a snarky comment about me being a part-timer. Somehow he restrained himself, turning to Tolland and saying, "Pete's going to be my lead investigator on this and Larry will assist him."

"Sounds good. I'm going to take the lead for our department. We're making it a priority, so resources won't be a problem, at least for a while. I'll have copies of what we have available for you anytime," he said to all of us.

"And I've got our original files on the cold cases," Dad added. He turned to us. "When you're done here, go check on her next of kin." He gave me the bagged license and I used my phone to take a picture of it.

Pete and I walked up and down the dirt road, looking for any clues before giving the location of the body one more look. "We can let the techs finish up here. We should see if we can find her family," I finally said.

"Guess we can't put it off any longer," Pete said reluctantly. We all hated to do next of kin notifications. "We'll drop my car off at the office and go in yours."

Pete liked me to drive so that he could text back and forth with his wife and daughters. I didn't mind. It was better than having him fidgeting in the driver's seat wanting to check the texts every time his phone buzzed, or worse, asking me to check them for him.

CHAPTER THIRTEEN

It was late afternoon by the time we got to Dawn's house. I'd asked dispatch for a records check which showed that the house was owned by a Bruce Littleton. I had no idea if he was a relation of Dawn's or if she rented the house. We knocked politely on the door, but there was no response. We knocked a little harder. Finally there were sounds of movement from inside.

When the door opened, a short man with spiked blond hair and an over-abundance of discount tattoos stood in the doorway looking annoyed. I immediately wished he could be our killer, but just by looking at him I could tell that he didn't have the brains or the motivation. Plus, he would have been about eight years old when the first murders took place.

"Jesus, aren't you two a little old to be Mormon missionaries?"

"Bruce?" Pete asked, moving his coat aside so the man could see his badge.

"He's our landlord."

"What's your name?"

"Andy."

We stared at him, waiting.

"Andy Bell," he finished grudgingly.

"Does Dawn Hall live here?" I asked.

"I don't know."

"What do you mean, you don't know? Don't you live here?" The man was really irritating.

"Yeah, I live here, but I think Dawn left me. She's been saying she would for weeks."

"Does Dawn have any family?" Pete pushed. I think he was finding the whiny gnome annoying too.

"Doesn't everybody? Come on, guys, I got things to do. What do you want?"

"What we want is an address or phone number for someone who cares about Dawn."

"I care. She just doesn't care about me. Witch hasn't called or texted me for days."

"You ever think maybe she couldn't?"

"What you mean?" He really seemed puzzled by this suggestion. "Like her phone won't work?"

"Can we come in?" I asked, then added, "We don't care about drugs or drug paraphernalia. But we might if you don't start cooperating."

"Hey, I don't have to let you in." He bowed up.

"No, but I bet Bruce might not mind giving us permission." I pulled out my phone and looked at him. "If we have to get Bruce's permission, we won't be happy. And unhappy deputies have very good eyesight. They see things that happy deputies might overlook." Of course, all of this was bluff. A landlord can't give the police permission to search a tenant's home. But sometimes a bluff is as good as a full house.

"Stop, stop, whatever, man," Andy said and backed into the house. Pete and I followed. The living room was disgusting. The carpet didn't look like it had ever been vacuumed and the walls were stained by years of tenants.

"Sorry, didn't have a chance to clean," he said, dropping down on the sagging couch. He still didn't seem concerned about Dawn.

"We need any information you have on Dawn's family."

"Ask her when you find her," he said dismissively.

"Look, you little snot, Dawn is dead," I tossed at him. Pete looked at me, a little surprised.

"What?" Andy sat up. For the first time, he seemed to be paying attention.

"We found Dawn's body this morning. Now, are you going to start cooperating?"

"Dead. Really? Damn." He seemed at a loss.

"We need to look through her things and we need some information from you."

"Okay. I guess. I never thought…" His voice trailed off.

"Information on her family?" Pete encouraged him.

"I… I don't know. I never met any of them. We've only been hanging out for a couple of months. Dawn needed a place to stay and I was living here. I just offered. Wasn't like we were a couple or anything. Fact, most of the time she slept in her own room. Called me a filthy pig." If the living room was any indication, I thought she'd hit the nail on the head.

"Come on, show us which room she used," I said.

"The one in the back," he said, pointing to a hallway that led off to the left.

"Did she have a cell phone?" Pete asked. The forensic team hadn't found one on her body.

"Everybody has a cell phone." He acted like we'd suggested she didn't have a mouth or eyes.

"Use yours to call her phone," I told him. Again he looked at me like I was speaking Greek, but he finally grabbed his phone off of the coffee table and pressed a few buttons. I listened and didn't hear anything. He turned the phone toward us.

"See, voicemail."

"Let me see that," Pete said, reaching his hand out for the phone. Reluctantly Andy handed it over. Pete copied Dawn's number into his phone and then casually scrawled through the text messages between Andy and Dawn. "We'll need to keep this," Pete told him.

Andy became animated for the first time since we'd met him. He rose up off the couch and came toward Pete.

"No way, man. No way. Give me my phone back." He was trying to reach out and take the phone from Pete. I got between them.

"This is how all of this is going to shake out. You're going to fully cooperate with our investigation. Right now we don't believe that you had anything to do with her death. And you really, really don't want us to change our minds."

"I know my rights." He said the first thing anyone who *doesn't* know their rights says. "You've got to have a warrant." He was still trying to reach past me and get his phone from Pete.

"We can do this one of three ways," I continued. "One, you give us permission and cooperate fully. We go that route and we're all friends working together to catch the bastard that killed Dawn. Two, we get a warrant, which will take about an hour and just piss us off. In that hour, we'll spend time arresting you for crap we can see out in the open. Remember, you did let us into the house. I see several drug-related items just from where I'm standing. The third way isn't much better than the second. We consider you a material witness and take you down to the sheriff's office for a formal interview while we get a warrant to search your premises for evidence. Friend or foe. Your choice. I'll count to three. One."

"You bastards. I got to have my phone. I do… I got stuff to do."

"I'm sure you do. Two. And the quickest way to get your life back to its bottom-feeder norm is to be our friend. Three. What's your decision?"

"Okay, okay. When can I get it back?" Andy begged.

"As a friend, I can tell you we'll return it as soon as we can."

"Probably a day, maybe two," Pete added.

"It's Friday," Andy said pitifully.

"I'm so sorry that Dawn's death is inconveniencing you,"

I said sarcastically. This guy really didn't bring out the best in me. "Now, friend, can we look over the room she slept in?"

"Yeah, whatever." He flopped back down on the couch and fell over, covering his face with a pillow. Pete rolled his eyes.

It was obvious which room Dawn spent most of her time in. It was the only one in the house that was clean and neat. The mattress and box spring sat directly on the floor, but the bed was made with care. There wasn't any other furniture in the room.

A small stack of books sat on the floor next to the bed. Some of the books were for school—biology and chemistry mostly. Beside the textbooks were a couple well-worn paperback historical romances. Two large suitcases were in the closet and the clothes that must have come out of them were neatly hung up or folded and placed in a row of cardboard boxes. I thought that Dawn would have been an easy person to like.

"Do you see an iPad or laptop?" I asked Pete.

"No, which is a little surprising. Maybe in her car?"

"Did she even have a car? Dispatch couldn't find any record of a car, but maybe it's registered in a parent's name. We'll have to ask the mushroom in the living room," I said, not really wanting to go deal with him again. "I wonder if we're wasting our time looking through her stuff. The killer might have just picked her out randomly after he failed to get Tonya."

"But we can't assume anything. For all we know, all of the murders were committed by different individuals. Ridiculous, but certainly any one of the victims, including Dawn, could have been killed by someone who knew her. Maybe when the killer couldn't get Tonya, he fell back and took someone he knew," Pete said.

I raised my hand. "I know, I know. And I realize that with a case this big, we have to be particularly careful about crossing t's and dotting i's," I admitted. "Let's go shake down that twerp in the other room and get some answers."

To my disgust, Andy was still lying on the couch with his head under the pillow. How proud his parents must have been. I kicked the couch. "Have you thought of any contacts?"

"She has a friend. Her name is Kelly. Kelly Baker. Her number's in my phone. She'll know all about Dawn's family," Andy said from under his pillow.

"Did Dawn have a car?" I asked the pillow.

"Yeah, a piece of crap. It's parked at the curb. But someone broke into it," Andy said.

I'd had enough and jerked the pillow away. "Why the hell didn't you tell us that earlier?"

"Cars are always getting trashed around here. Hell, it would have been more surprising if it hadn't been broken into," he grumbled.

"Come on. Show us her car," I ordered. He groaned, but my tone told him that arguing with me right now would be a mistake.

We followed him outside. In front of the house next door was a ten-year-old blue Toyota with its window busted out.

"Why didn't she park in the driveway?" Pete asked.

"I had some friends over for a little party Saturday."

Pete and I walked around the car. The back passenger window facing away from the street was the one that was broken, but there were pieces of plastic on the ground near the driver's window. I knelt down and looked under the car. Halfway under was a broken laptop. Several coins and a tube of lipstick were next to the tire. I also found some Kleenex and other debris that might have come from a woman's handbag.

"Dawn dropped her purse and her laptop here," I told Pete, who pulled out his radio and called for a patrol officer and crime scene techs.

"Look here." Pete had gone back to looking over the car. He was pointing to a spot on the driver's side between the front and back windows.

"That's blood."

"Looks like it. You figure someone else broke into the car after she was abducted?" he asked.

"In this neighborhood, yep. And they probably took her purse or bag."

"She dropped it when she was attacked and some scavenger picked it up later."

It was dark and the temperature was dropping by the time the techs showed up. Pete agreed to stay and secure the scene and get the car towed in while I interviewed Kelly Baker and tried to get a line on Dawn's next of kin.

Andy was sitting in his front yard, watching everything. I went over to him.

"I'll call you when you can pick up your phone. No, wait. Can't do that because I'll have your phone," I teased him, a little cruelly. But I pulled out a card and dropped it on the ground next to him. "There's my number. Call me on Monday and I'll let you know when you can get your phone." He didn't say anything and I walked away.

When I got in touch with Kelly Baker, she was getting ready to go out for the evening. I told her I was with the Adams County Sheriff's Office and needed to speak with her about Dawn. She started to ask questions, but I told her I'd rather explain everything in person and asked her to wait for me.

While I was on the way to Kelly's house I got a call from a TV reporter, wanting to know the name of the victim. I told her that the family hadn't been notified, but that we were working on it and should be able to give it to them for the eleven o'clock news. No doubt, Dad had given them my number.

Kelly lived with her parents in a very nice home on the edge of town.

"What's this all about?" she asked, opening the door for me to come in. She had high cheekbones and dark hair, like a teenage Jacqueline Kennedy, though her attire was more

Britney Spears than Mrs. Kennedy.

"You're friends with Dawn Hall?" I purposefully used the present tense, but she was smart enough to know that we didn't visit people's friends for overdue parking tickets.

"What's happened?" She'd forgotten she had someplace to go. Dawn had better taste in girlfriends than roommates.

"Could we sit down? I'm afraid this is very bad news, and I have a few questions."

Wordlessly, she showed me into the living room, which adjoined the dining room where her mother, father and brother were sitting at the table. Her parents quit eating and stared at me. I sat in a chair while Kelly sat across from me on the sofa.

"I'm afraid we found Dawn's body this morning. It appears that someone killed her," I said as gently as possible.

"Oh, no," Kelly said. "I told her she should move in with us. That neighborhood is sooo bad. And that guy is worthless." She bit her lip and hit the cushion next to her. Her mom came over and sat beside her on the sofa. Kelly leaned against her mom's shoulder.

"Dawn was a wonderful girl," Kelly's mother said sadly.

"We need to contact her family," I said.

"She doesn't have much family. Kelly went to high school with her, and she was living with her aunt then," the older woman said, cradling her daughter.

"Her dad died of a heart attack when she was in middle school and her mom had already been diagnosed with cancer. She fought it and lived until Dawn's junior year. I can't believe this." Tears were flowing down Kelly's cheeks.

"What about her aunt?"

"She moved over to Jacksonville and got married a year ago. Dawn and I went to the wedding. She'll be devastated." Kelly gave me an address for the aunt. She didn't have her phone number.

"When was the last time you talked to Dawn?"

"Saturday. She was going to go to her job at Roma's in Tallahassee. Dawn was working her way through college. She refused to take out loans. She'd work and save up, go to school for a semester or two, then take time off from school to work full time again and save more money."

"Is it unusual for you not to hear from her for a week?"

"Dawn was a very independent person. She called when she needed to call, but not to chit chat. And we'd gotten into some arguments lately. I thought she was being stubborn about money. Living with that cretin to save on rent. I told her I didn't think that was smart."

I didn't get much more out of Kelly, who was still crying and had cancelled her plans for the evening by the time I left. The folks in dispatch were able to dig up a phone number for Dawn's aunt, and I was finally able to deliver the grim news. Like Kelly predicted, the woman sounded broken-hearted over the death of her niece.

CHAPTER FOURTEEN

I finally headed for home at eight o'clock, but I didn't make it. Dad called and asked me to stop by his house. Luckily I didn't have any plans with Cara that night as we were going to spend Saturday afternoon together, but Ivy would give me hell for being so late with her dinner.

When I pulled through the gate at Dad's place I saw that the light was on in the barn, Dad's silhouette going back and forth between Mac and Finn's stalls. Ivy wasn't the only one being fed late tonight. I helped him put out two piles of hay in the paddock and gave each of the horses a couple of alfalfa cubes as we turned them loose for the night. They'd both earned my respect last month when they'd managed to remain sane while the world went crazy around them.

Dad and I headed back to the house. He walked a bit more stiffly these days, but no less proudly. When we got to the door, he stopped and turned to me. "Go in by yourself," he told me with a prankster's glint in his green eyes.

"Why? What's up with Mauser?" I asked suspiciously, wondering if the joke was going to be on the dog or me.

"That big lout's had his dinner and I bet he's snoring away on the couch. I just think he needs a little lesson about sleeping while on guard duty."

"Do you really think the he needs a shock to the ticker like that?" I joked. It was good seeing Dad this relaxed. The last couple of months had been hard on all of us, and I still wasn't sure how the resurfacing of an old nemesis was going to affect him.

"Go on."

I opened the door and walked through the kitchen. I could hear the giant snoring as soon as I entered the house. I made it halfway across the living room before his head bounced up off of the couch and he let out a window-rattling bark. For a moment he wasn't sure who I was and the hair along his back stood up while a low growl came from deep in his throat. In those few seconds, the look he gave me caused my stomach to tighten, but in a flash it was over. He recognized me, gave me a couple happy *how are you?* barks, wallowed his way off of the couch and threw himself against my legs.

"He could have been a burglar or a murderer, you lazy dog," Dad playfully chastised the black-and-white Dane. Mauser just danced for joy. Finally, after a couple unearned treats, the monster settled down on the floor of the living room, his head across Dad's feet.

"You're in a good mood," I told Dad, sitting down across from him.

"Yes, I am. A chance to close unfinished business. Not that I'm happy we've had two murders. Don't get me wrong. But for sixteen years I've felt like the bastard was out there, laughing at us. Now I've got another chance to get him."

"He grabbed Dawn outside her house. It was only two blocks away from the Sweet Spot."

"I just wish Tonya had gotten a good look at him. Is there any chance?"

"I don't think so. The old man was pretty sure that she didn't see the blow coming. And Ray's not expected to survive much longer. His body is failing."

"Bad luck all around. But we'll get him."

"Why are you so confident? Not getting on your case, but

if you couldn't catch him sixteen years ago…"

"He's given us a lot better chance this time. With the killings spread over such a long gap of time, we can use that to eliminate suspects. We had about a hundred persons of interests that we narrowed down to twenty-five likely suspects last time. We'll start with those and a lot of them can be eliminated pretty easily now. They're either dead, they've moved, or they're not able to commit the murders for other reasons—health, alibis, whatever. It's simply easier to catch a serial killer who kills in locations that are separated by place or time. Of course, that's after you make the connection that the same killer is at work."

Dad got up and went to the dining room table, picking up a list with almost a hundred names on it and handing it to me. "I made a copy of the original list of one hundred. I didn't want to take a chance that we were wrong when we narrowed the list to twenty-five. He might not even be on that list at all, but I think it's a good start."

I looked over the names. I don't know why, but I was surprised when I recognized some of them. "Pete and I will start on them tomorrow," I said, thinking that my plans to spend the day with Cara were going down the drain fast. At least with this case, we didn't have to wait for current forensic data from the labs because we could start by reviewing all the information that had been collected previously. Just reading and comparing all of the old information would take time.

"I need to go. Ivy's waiting for me."

He nodded and walked me out to my car.

I texted Pete Saturday morning and we agreed to meet at Winston's Grill. I drove by Dr. Barnhill's on the way and was rewarded with the sight of Cara outside walking a sulky-looking English Bulldog. I parked the car and walked over to them.

"You don't look very happy," I told the Bulldog

Cara gave me a wide smile, then turned her attention back to the dog. "His parents had to go out of town and Gorignak is not a big fan of our resort. Even though he gets all kinds of special attention," she said, frowning down at the stocky beast.

"I gotta ask,,, Gorignak?"

"The rock monster from *Galaxy Quest*. His owners are big-time geeks. He goes by Nakie for short. Nakie, which rhymes with snackie." He looked up at her as soon as he heard the word snackie. "Not for you, chubbo," she told him.

"Ouch, tough love. I'm on my way to meet Pete."

"There's a front page article on the *Tallahassee Democrat's* website about the body they found. Is there really a serial killer here in Adams County?"

"He's been here for more than fifteen years."

"That's what the article said. I guess our afternoon together is off, huh?" I appreciated that she didn't make it sound like a complaint.

"I'm sorry." I apologized anyway.

"No worries. I wish I could help."

"Just stay safe." We kissed lightly and I bent down to pet Nakie before heading off to meet Pete.

The parking lot at Winston's was full. Not surprising. I'm sure that half the folks there wanted to talk about the latest Swamp Hacker killing. Pete was already making inroads into his rancher breakfast, which included three eggs, bacon, hash browns and a short stack of pancakes.

"Dieting today?" I couldn't help kidding him, but I worried about him sometimes.

"Hey, everyone has their vices. Gluttony is mine. The people you have to worry about are the ones who don't wear their vices out in public." He pointed his fork at me and arched his eyebrows.

"Stupidity is mine. And I think everyone is well aware of it," I informed him. I took out the list Dad had given me and placed it upside down on the table so that prying eyes at other tables wouldn't get a look at it. Pete put his fork down and picked it up.

"Dad gave that to me last night. A little over a hundred names that they were looking at last time around."

Mary walked up to the table with her pad in hand. I was glad to see a familiar face after my last visit.

"Not cooking today?" I asked her. Mary's dad, the owner of the Grill and its namesake, had recently let her move up from waiting tables to cooking.

"No, Dad felt like coming in and taking over the spatula this morning." She smiled broadly as she poured my coffee. Mary had been a bit worried about her father lately. Her mother had left them last year and she'd felt that he was letting his depression get the best of him.

"Glad he's doing better," I told her. "I'll take a short stack. Maple syrup." She jotted it down and left.

Pete and I decided that we'd split up the list and try to eliminate as many of the names as we could. We also needed to go through the forensic evidence from sixteen years ago. We'd need to take some of it to Dr. Darzi so that he could compare the cases to the latest victims. Leon County had already given him their records after they made the connection to the first victim. In theory, what they had from the previous cases should have been the same as what we had, but theory ain't fact.

Pete looked around the restaurant. "Everyone's talking about it. Maybe we'll get lucky and someone will remember something."

"Which reminds me. We need to organize a canvass of the neighborhood between the Sweet Spot and Dawn's house."

"That'll be fun. How many doors can we get slammed in our faces in one day?" Pete asked sarcastically, but then he thought about it for a moment. "Or maybe not. When they learn that this predator is stalking their streets, we might get some cooperation."

"A few of our deputies have a good relationship with the

community. I'll get with them. If they're part of the group, we might stand a chance of reaching folks."

"Tomorrow's Sunday. After church would be good. Everyone will have heard about it by then."

"And that'll give us some time to put it together," I said, starting in on the pancakes Mary had brought me. I'd sort of come to prefer her cooking to her dad's, but I was glad he was getting himself back together. I saw him come out front to talk to a couple of customers and he waved to Pete as we were paying.

Back at the office we carried the files from the first attacks into a conference room where we could spread everything out on the table. Then we split the list in half and started going through the names. Beside each name was a list of the suspect's vital statistics. All of the suspects were thirty or over at the time.

"Why not any younger suspects?"

"They were going by this." I held up an official profile report that they had received from the FBI. "Standard stuff. White male, between thirty and forty, probably not married, possible record of animal abuse and/or arson, may be disfigured or have a speech impediment, possible anger management issues, probably has a working-class job." I read the list quickly.

"Agents get paid for that? These days with computers they can just copy and paste it in response to any request they get."

"Hey, they might have to make some changes. There wasn't any sex involved with these murders, so they couldn't say anything about... Oh wait, I missed it. Here it is—possible sexual performance issues. You're right. The job's not much different than a fortune teller. Make it all vague enough and when they catch the guy you can point out how right you were."

"We'd better quit criticizing other people's work and do our own," Pete said.

It was a long process of phone calls and checking public

records.

"I'm down to fifteen still in town and seemingly in good health," I said.

"I've only got ten left. Ten of mine are in jail for other crimes, some moved, some are dead, five of those from drug overdoses. So twenty-five names. We should go through the files and pull out the names of some of the younger people associated with the crimes. I'm not buying the original assumption about his age."

"I agree. That's going to take a while. We can pull in a few more people to help," I suggested.

"How much of this do you think is available digitally?" Pete asked, looking at the piles of case records.

"If it was just our department, I'd think that a lot of it wouldn't be. But Leon County was the lead, so I'd say a fair amount."

I picked up the phone, called their office and asked to speak with Tolland. There was hesitation until I mentioned which case I was working on. He was on the phone in a couple of minutes. First thing he did was give me his cell phone number.

"How are you all doing?" He didn't seem at all surprised that we were working on a Saturday.

"We're going through a list of names that Dad gave me. We've eliminated most of them. Would you all have been using the same list?"

"Not originally. But your dad and I corrected that as soon as he became sheriff. It was one of the first things he wanted to do. He and I spent a couple of weekends going over everything and trying to synchronize the two investigations. Sixteen years ago we had a couple of sheriffs who didn't really get along, so they kept a tight rein on us. Didn't want to share everything. But your dad and I fixed that. The list he gave you would be the one that he and I put together."

"How much of the records has been digitalized?"

"Most of it. Ted and I had the paper reports from Adams

County scanned in when we went over everything."

"We've scheduled the autopsy for Monday morning. I talked to Darzi, and he didn't see any need to rush it. He did pull some samples to begin the lab work," I said.

"I'll be there."

I started to tell him the assumptions we were making in putting together a suspect list, but he interrupted me. "I'd rather we go our own ways for now and then get together and compare notes in a few days. That way there's less chance that we'll get into… What do they call it? Group think or a feedback loop?"

I was beginning to understand why Dad had so much respect for Tolland. I told him we'd see him Monday and hung up.

"Why were you so interested in getting all the files online?" I asked Pete.

"I thought we might ask one of the IT guys to put them all together and do a word search. I'd be interested in the names that come up most often."

"I get it. Killers, particularly publicity-seeking killers, often hover around the investigation."

"Exactly. Is there someone whose name pops up repeatedly as a witness or inquiring after one of the victims or volunteering information? That sort of thing."

"For now, do you want to start visiting some of the suspects? A few of them are bound to have airtight alibis for Dawn's murder. That's another advantage we have over the original investigation. They never had a solid time frame for any of the murders. The closest they came was the double murder, when they were able to narrow it down to a six-hour period."

"We can't be sure when the body was placed in the woods," Pete said.

I thought about that. "True, but it's hard to imagine him keeping the body around any longer than he had to," I argued. Pete just shrugged. "And it doesn't matter. We *do* have the window of time when he assaulted Tonya and

Dawn. Any of the remaining suspects who have a solid alibi for that time period can be eliminated."

We split the list of suspects. I took the extra one, leaving me with lucky thirteen.

CHAPTER FIFTEEN

It was a beautiful day, cool and sunny. I would have given anything to be spending the afternoon with Cara, but at least this didn't feel like a waste of time. Hunting a serial killer is very different from a lot of law enforcement work. It feels urgent, like a clock is ticking and someone's life depends on your ability to hunt down and stop the predator before he feels the need to kill again.

Four people on my list weren't home, and two had moved without changing the address on their driver's license. I was able to eliminate another man who worked for a cable service company that could verify his whereabouts for the time of the assault. That left me with six names.

The first lived only a mile from the Sweet Spot, in a middle-class home in a small subdivision. The door was answered by a man wearing jogging shorts and a T-shirt. He looked like he'd been on a week-long bender.

"What do you want?" he asked, his eyes hooded and cold.

"I want to speak with Tom West."

"You got him. Same question. What do you want?"

"I'm an investigator with the Adams County Sheriff's Office." I'd decided that explaining my reserve status wasn't worth the time or possible confusion. "I'd like to ask you a few questions."

"So ask."

"Can I come in?"

"Not until I find out what this is all about," he answered.

I hated being treated like a magazine salesman. "I'm looking into the recent murders of two young women."

"The Swamp Hacker murders, part two. Why didn't you say so? You all wasted your time the first go 'round looking at innocent guys like me, and now you're going around that bush one more time? Hell, you're too young to have even been on the original cases. What right do you have coming around here and talking that crap to me?" He stared straight into my eyes, challenging me to question him.

"This is not the best the way to get yourself off the persons of interest list," I reasoned.

"Maybe I like being on it." His eyes did an odd, crazy roll. "Like it more than talking to some wet-behind-the-ears detective wannabe."

Tom's eyes met mine for a second then went off again on their own trip looking for who knew what. He wasn't any taller than me, though standing in the door gave him an additional six inches. He weighed a good twenty pounds more, but that was all in the gut. I figured he was all bluff, but with a little touch of crazy.

"Fine. You don't have to answer my questions, but that just means I'll have to go around to all your neighbors and ask them if they remember seeing you last Saturday night." His eyes darted to mine and actually held steady. Maybe I finally had his attention. "And when I get done doing that, I'll go around to your place of business and ask your co-workers if they know anything."

That got him. His eyes shifted left, right and then down to the ground. "Screw you."

"Your choice."

"Oh, hell," he said and walked back into his house, leaving the door open for me.

The inside of the house was a man-hovel. Andy, Dawn's roommate, would have felt right at home.

"I've been pissed off for sixteen years about the way they treated me. I should have sued their asses off. Treated me like a suspect when I didn't know anything about those killings," he said, waving his arms around dramatically.

"Why do you think they considered you a suspect?" I'd skimmed over the file and the transcript of the interviews with him. They'd done a pretty good job spelling out the reason he was on that list. He had known almost all of the victims, he had owned a truck that burned mysteriously after he was interviewed the first time and he was known to be a generally odd person.

"A bunch of bullshit. I got in fights. I told people off. So what?"

"You knew most of the victims," I stated.

"So what? They weren't much younger than me. More like I knew their families. My dad was a damn good mechanic, and I worked with him. I met a lot of people at the shop. Like I said, I knew some of them because I went to school with their older brothers. I grew up here."

"Where were you last Saturday night?"

"I need another alibi? I don't know. Here, maybe." His anger had changed quickly to helplessness. The rapid mood changes didn't make me feel better about him. But then some people just have issues; it doesn't mean they're killers.

"That's not very convincing."

"I don't have to prove my innocence. You have to prove my guilt. Isn't that how it works?"

"That's how it works. But it's a lot easier and saves a lot of time if you have a provable alibi that checks out."

"I didn't know I'd need one," he said, which was the most convincing statement he'd made.

"What aren't you telling me?" I asked.

"Nothing. I'm done."

"Look, if you have a good but embarrassing alibi, just lay it out on the table and we can be done with this."

He didn't say anything and he didn't move.

"Even if it's illegal, if it's a victimless crime and is unconnected to the murders, I have no interest in pursuing it."

Tom considered my offer for a moment. "I visit a lady every Saturday night. Especially since my wife ran off a couple years ago."

"The same lady?" I was professional and nonjudgmental.

"Usually."

"Last Saturday?"

"Yeah."

"What's her name and do you have a phone number where I can reach her?"

"You're going to laugh," he said, looking down at the carpet and speaking very softly.

"Try me."

"Trixie, she goes by the name Trixie."

It was a pretty dumb nickname for a prostitute. A little too much on the nose. But I didn't laugh as I wrote down the name and number he gave me.

"I'll check it out," I said, then moved on.

The other guy who interested me was nice. Too nice.

He lived in an upscale home on five acres. The house was brick and the yard immaculate. When I knocked on the door, his wife answered. She was as well trimmed as the house and yard, wearing a bit too much makeup for my taste.

"Hello!" she greeted me. Her Southern accent was almost as heavy as the makeup. "Come on in," she said, before I even had a chance to tell her who I was and why I was there.

I followed her to the living room. Throw pillows were everywhere and the air smelled of one too many scented candles.

"I need to talk with Tony Stevenson," I told her.

"I'm Mrs. Stevenson. Tony's working on the back patio. I'll just go get him. Can I get you something to drink?"

I told her I was fine and watched her sashay out of the room.

Tony came in wearing colorful checked shorts and a salmon-colored polo shirt. I knew that he was over forty-five, but he looked like he was thirty. Tall and slim, he extended his hand toward me before he was halfway across the room.

"Tony Stevenson. How can I help you?" His smile was large and appeared genuine.

I shook his hand, realizing that all the Southern hospitality had effectively disarmed me. I felt myself wearing a smile that I didn't really want to be there.

"I'm Larry Macklin, an investigator with the Adams County Sheriff's Office. I wanted to ask you a few questions."

"Sure. Sit down." His smile was still firmly in place as he waved me toward the sofa. I had to move pillows to find room to sit.

Tony perched on a chair across from me, leaning forward with his eyes directly on mine as though he couldn't wait to find out what questions I wanted to ask him and was eager to answer them. But just as I was about to start, he raised a finger.

"I know what this is about. I had some run-ins with the law when I was a kid. Kind of wild. Gave my parents fits. I remember that the police looked at me when those killings took place years ago. Seems crazy now. But well, I can't blame them. So go ahead and ask me what you need to."

His record included an assault when he was in his twenties that had left a man badly injured and several arrests for drunk and disorderly conduct. He had also been accused of threatening a girlfriend with a baseball bat.

"I'm glad you understand our need to be thorough." Again I found myself smiling at this man for no reason. "Where were you last Saturday night?"

"Where I am most nights, here at home. My wife will vouch for that."

I bet she would. But I wouldn't bet he was here. Something was very off in this house. His life had too much makeup on it.

"What type of car do you own?"

"We have several. A minivan. It's aspirational—we don't have any children yet, but we're still trying. That's my wife's car. We've also got a Lexus and a Dodge pickup. Out here in the country, you've got to have a pickup."

I made notes. "Thank you. That's all for now." I didn't see any reason to ask his wife to confirm his alibi. Maybe if we had some solid evidence, but I'd want to take her out of this Stepford house before I questioned her. I stood up.

"Sure I can't get you a drink?" Tony offered.

"No, thanks. I have more folks to interview."

"Good luck. It's awful what some people are capable of." He always said the most socially acceptable thing.

The remaining interviews were pretty commonplace. The men I met were mostly down on their luck with old criminal records that guaranteed they would never do any better.

I called Pete and compared notes. He had a couple men who would stay on the suspect list, but most of the rest no longer fit anyone's profile of a serial killer. We hashed out some of the details concerning the next day's canvassing of the area around the Sweet Spot and Dawn's house. I told him I wanted to talk with Dawn's co-workers at Roma's. Leon County had already contacted them, but I still wanted to talk to anyone there who knew her.

I called Cara and asked her if she wanted to go on a working date with me. When she heard where I was planning to go, she didn't hesitate. She had a soft spot for Italian food.

I ran home first to change and to feed Ivy. There was no way was I going to be late with her dinner two days in a row.

I picked up Cara just before dark. She'd called ahead for reservations. "A real date on a Saturday night," she said, smiling as she got into the car. She was wearing a dark green sweater dress that complimented her red hair and her deep blue eyes were sparkling.

"Well, I do need to interview some of the staff," I said apologetically.

"Just don't make anyone mad before we get our food." Cara gave me a light punch on the arm. "How's the investigation going?" she asked, some of the humor leaving her voice.

"It's early days yet, but this is going to be difficult. I'm not used to working a murder where motive isn't a factor."

"It's all just random?"

"Appears to be. Predator is the right word for a serial killer. They live among us and when they feel the urge, they just pick a victim based on looks, availability and timing. In most murders, motive is the driving force. But for a serial killer, opportunity is the most important consideration." I thought about it for a moment, then added, "And the urge."

"The urge?"

"The impulse. I think that goes hand-in-hand with opportunity. Imagine you're walking through the kitchen and someone has put out a plate of chocolate chip cookies. You know they don't want you eating them, but when you see them you get the urge, the desire for one of them. If the person is standing right there watching you, then you don't have the opportunity. But if they leave you alone with the cookies, then the desire combined with the opportunity means one less cookie on the tray."

"Or two or three. Unless you have impulse control."

"Exactly, and a lack of impulse control is a defining feature of a serial killer."

"And they don't kill all the time because they don't always have the urge when they have the opportunity?" Cara asked thoughtfully.

"Like walking through that kitchen, but your mind is on things other than cookies."

"Chocolate chip cookies are always a high priority for me."

"Maybe cookies were a bad example." I smiled and got another light punch on the arm.

I was glad Cara had called ahead. The parking lot was almost full. The weather was perfect, with a chill and the smell of wood smoke in the air. Half a dozen people were waiting for tables around the maître d's station. I gave the woman my name and she told me that it would be a few minutes while they cleared a table.

"I'm going to go ahead and see if I can talk to the manager," I told Cara and she promised to get our table if it was ready before I got back.

I exchanged a few words with an officious looking fellow in a black vest with a name tag that read: *Alberto*, though I was guessing that Albert was closer to the truth. He told me he was the assistant manager and would be glad to talk with me, though he was also quick to remind me that they were busy. I felt a little guilty about that. He took me into a private room that was being set for a large party.

"You said this was about Dawn. It's horrible," he said as soon as the door closed.

"She waited tables?"

"Sometimes she was a hostess, but she liked waiting tables best."

"How long had she worked here?"

"I don't know exactly. About a year."

"Was she a good employee?"

"The best. I wish everyone was like her. Dawn did her work. She was friendly to everyone, but she didn't get into any of the catty kitchen stuff like a lot of the girls and, honestly, the guys. A lot of waiters are gossips at heart."

"Did she have any particular friends?"

"Not really. She lived over in Adams County and, once we were done and the tips were divided up, she was usually in a hurry to get home. Always afraid her car wouldn't make it. A couple times it didn't.

"One time that creature she called her roommate dropped her off. Yuck." He made a face. "I really don't know what else to tell you. She came in, she worked, everyone liked her, and she went home. A few times she talked about how hard it was working her way through school. I remember she was going to be a nurse. Damn, how sad is that?"

He seemed touched by her death. Not deeply like you would be for a close friend or family member, but like when you see something beautiful that's been destroyed for no reason. Which, from all appearances, was exactly what had happened. He gave me a few names of employees that were on familiar terms with Dawn, but said he didn't think any of them had ever had contact with her outside of work. One of them was working that night, so Alberto sent her back to talk with me and she said essentially the same things he did.

"Did you talk to everyone you needed to?" Cara asked me when I joined her at our table.

"Yep, and I heard what I expected to hear. Dawn was a great employee who was pleasant and kept to herself."

"So awful. No one deserves to die like that, but it seems like the killer was determined to take out wonderful people. Tonya and then Dawn."

"Luckily Tonya is going to recover. The doctors are expecting her to regain consciousness in a couple of days. I don't think Shantel has left the hospital through this whole ordeal."

"You said Tonya won't remember anything."

"I doubt it, though I don't think she saw anything. Dawn either. That's this maniac's MO. Come up behind—" The waiter came and took our orders. When he left, I said, "We don't need to be talking about this at dinner."

"Don't worry. I hate that it happened, but I'm glad you're working on the case."

"I'm not sure how I feel about it. I was ready to give up being an investigator."

"Having doubts? We've been over this. I'll support you as long as it's what you want, and you don't shut me out."

"I don't know. Maybe it's just this case. The danger that

this man represents. I understand why my father was so obsessed with catching him."

"I like your father."

"That's good. Don't they say that if you want to know how the son will turn out, look at the father? Oh, no, what am I saying?"

Cara grinned. "They say the same about mothers and daughters."

"Your mother's okay."

She laughed. "Just okay? So I'll just be okay?"

"You are already much more than okay," I said, reaching across the table to take her hand.

"Seriously, your dad is great. He's funny when he's around Mauser or the horses."

"He's always loved animals. He's usually too indulgent with them. For me, Dad was not the easiest father to grow up with. When he paid attention to me it was usually way too intense, but more often than not, he was preoccupied with his work. Mom made everything all right. She always knew when I needed him, and she'd have a word with him. He loved her so much that he'd do whatever she asked. I've told you that's why he became sheriff. She joked with him for years about running for sheriff. None of us took it seriously."

"It must have been hard for both of you when she died."

"Dad went days without speaking to me. Not because he was being cruel. He was just so lost inside himself that it never occurred to him that he needed to talk to me."

"Still, you suggested he run for office."

"I wasn't sure he'd do it. I think what finally tipped the scale was a birthday card he found. Mom had drawn it. It was pretty childish—she wasn't an artist, but it was just for fun. It said: *To Ted, my sheriff, the man who wears the star.* Seeing it in her handwriting, the word 'sheriff' seemed to move him. Once he got it into his head that that's what she would have wanted, there was no stopping him. For months, whenever he was off duty, he'd drive to a neighborhood and knock on

116

every door and listen to anyone who would talk to him. He won the election handily."

Cara smiled at me and squeezed my hand. Then the waiter delivered our food and we were both distracted by the excellent aroma and taste. We ate until we were stuffed, but we managed to share cannoli for dessert.

We drove back to Adams County in companionable silence. Then I turned the radio to a classic rock station and we both sang along like a couple of silly kids. For just a moment, I was able to stop thinking about the hunt that lay ahead.

CHAPTER SIXTEEN

I woke up Sunday morning alone. Well, almost alone. Ivy was sitting on the bed, staring into my face from six inches away and using all of her feline mind control powers to make me get up and feed her breakfast. Once she realized that mind control was failing, she resorted to reaching out and kneading my pillow while purring loud enough to penetrate my dreamless sleep. I opened one eye.

"Really?" I looked over at the clock, which told me it was almost eight-thirty. I sighed. "Okay, okay." I crawled out of bed reluctantly and fed the princess her breakfast.

Pete and I had scheduled a meeting with a few patrol deputies for one o'clock to review the questions we wanted them to ask while canvassing the neighborhood around the Sweet Spot and Dawn's house. I decided to use the morning to go over the old files and come up with criteria for expanding our list of suspects to males who were as young as twenty years old when the original murders took place. I had some of the information that had been used to develop the original suspect list. I wanted to go over that and see what criteria, besides age, should have been considered so that we could cast a net wide enough to catch the killer, but not so wide that he was obscured by red herrings.

I was using my desktop to access the office database and trying to see how the online files on the original case were organized when I got a text message.

Hola from Miami! It was from Eddie Thompson, my confidential, cross-dressing informant. He'd saved my life twice, at least according to him, and had felt the need to flee the county when everything blew up with his family last month.

Me: *Having fun?*

Eddie: *It's crazy fun here. But like Dorothy said, there's no place like home.*

Me: *Only your dad and Edwards are still in jail. Rest made bail.*

Eddie: *Yeah, word is Gramps is running things. He never liked me. I'll keep dancing on South Beach! Heard the Swamp Hacker is back. Insane. Good luck with that.*

Me: *Thanks. You better go. Your gramps might be intercepting our texts.*

Eddie: *Shit, didn't think about that. Later.*

Okay, that last was a little cruel, but all in good fun.

As I reviewed the old records, I thought about the characteristics of a serial killer. Having a record of violent behavior toward women was number one. Second was anti-social behavior, third was arson and the fourth, animal cruelty. The prime demographics were male, white, thirty to forty-five years old. Since several of our victims had been African Americans, did that mean that that a black man could have committed these crimes? Black serial killers are as rare as hen's teeth, but they do exist. The D.C. sniper and Wayne Williams, who killed children in Atlanta, were two. And some who were never caught, such as the phantom in Texarkana, might have been black. It was something to consider.

My phone rang.

"She woke up. And it's Sunday." The joy in Shantel's voice made me smile.

"I'm really glad she's doing better."

"I can breathe again. Praise God, I can breathe again."

"Would you like to help us find this guy?"

"Hell, yes," she said, her voice deep and serious. "Just tell me what I can do."

"Take today and be with Tonya, but tomorrow, if you can, start going over the evidence from the earlier cases and cross-reference it with what we've gotten this time. We want to expand the suspect list. Tolland with Leon County will help you access their records."

"I'm itching to get on that SOB's trail."

I assured her we'd get him and told her to call me if she had any problems tomorrow.

Just gathering the data that we needed to expand our list was going to be challenging and time consuming. And for both the original list and our expanded list, there was a major piece of the puzzle that was out of reach. Juvenile records are sealed. Our killer may have gotten into trouble for abusing people or animals or for arson when under eighteen, but if he wasn't adjudicated as an adult, then we'd never know.

My hyperactive phone rang again. It was Pete this time, confirming that we'd meet with the other deputies at Winston's Grill. Some of them were working off the clock so he'd offered everyone lunch.

"You paying?" I joked.

"We'll go halfsies. This is our case."

When I got there, Winston himself was waiting our table. There was one male and two female deputies. Julio joined us a few minutes after I sat down. Everyone ordered a large meal at our expense.

"You all eat like that, all you're going to want to do is curl up somewhere and take a nap," I grumbled good-naturedly.

"I caught that one sleeping in his patrol car last week," Teresa Pelham said, pointing playfully at Derick Jacobs.

"That's bull. I was typing up a report," Derick said, trying to defend himself.

"I tapped on his window with my flashlight and he practically jumped through the roof of the car."

"You startled me."

The joking and jostling went on until Pete raised his hand. "Okay, now that most of you all are done eating, let's remember that you're here for a reason. Larry and I have drawn up a list of questions we want you to go over with anyone who will answer their door."

"I think we'll have some luck. Just cruising through there the last couple of days, people have wanted to talk. Some of them are pretty scared," Julio stated.

"Good. I'm scared. Everyone should be. There's a freak out there killing people and hacking them up," Pete said, a little louder than some of the after-church-on-Sunday families eating lunch around us would have preferred.

Winston came by with coffee. "It's crazy. Everyone who comes in here's scared," he said to the table at large. Everyone nodded as he filled our cups.

Pete handed out the list of questions and copies of a map that showed everyone's assignments. "I know you all could have done a good job without us telling you what to ask, but we want to be thorough and consistent," he said.

The questions were mostly of the *have you seen anything* variety. Have you seen a strange car or truck hanging out in the neighborhood? On Saturday? If so, what did it look like? Could you see the driver? If so, what did he look like? What time was it? That sort of thing.

"This could take a while," said Susan White, a large and intimidating black officer with a disarming smile. She reminded me of an elementary school teacher I'd had. If that woman frowned in your direction, you would wet your pants. But if she smiled at one of your answers, you felt like the whole world loved you.

"Yep, so we should get started," Pete told everyone.

"Just one thing before we go," I said. "I know I don't have to remind you all that Shantel's niece was attacked by this guy. I know this one feels personal for all of us. Push people, but don't push them into an answer that isn't true."

Everyone nodded solemnly. They knew how easy it could

be to guide a witness. Far too easy. Even when you didn't want to, you could end up getting answers you wanted rather than answers that were true. But looking around the table, I felt good about our prospects. This group represented some of the best and most dedicated deputies in the department.

As we were leaving, Winston offered free pie and coffee if we wanted to come back when we were done. It sounded like a deal to all of us, so we agreed to meet back there at five.

We all were pretty much done-in by the time we got back to the restaurant. True to his word, Winston had a couple of strawberry pies waiting for us, made with fruit fresh from Plant City. We agreed to eat pie first and compare notes later.

With both pies and about a gallon of coffee gone, we all leaned forward and swapped notes. All of us had talked with people who'd seen suspicious cars, trucks or vans that they wanted us to look into. Only a handful sounded promising and had enough information to be useful.

"You're going to love this," Susan said. "Mohammed Attica gave me a very detailed description of a truck he saw driving through the neighborhood."

"Oh, lord," Julio groaned.

Mohammed was a self-proclaimed community leader. Though he tended to bring a lot of bluster and drama in his wake, he truly did care about the people in his community and, every once in a blue moon, came up with a tip that was really important. Of course, he had also filed half a dozen civil suits against various county agencies, including one against the sheriff's office that Dad still hadn't forgiven him for, even though the suit had been dismissed. Dad had wasted a week of work digging up a bunch of evidence and providing it to the county attorney.

"What did he see?" Despite his reputation, I wasn't passing up anyone's help.

"A black Ford pickup. He called it a redneck truck. The guy driving it was white and wore a ball cap. He saw it parked about a block from his house. He thought that was on Friday and then he's pretty sure he saw the same truck Saturday evening. Maybe around eight, he said. No tag. Maybe he could pick the guy out of a lineup, but he had no idea how tall or how much the guy weighed since he only saw him in the truck. When pressed, he said the guy probably wasn't obese or super skinny."

There were possibilities there. Maybe the guy was cruising for victims, or he was a construction worker who'd been paid on Friday and was looking for drugs, or he was just a stalky ex-boyfriend. But it was information that might come in handy and Pete wrote it all down.

We moved on to Julio, who had information on a van parked by the side of the road down from the Sweet Spot, possibly on Saturday. The woman who saw it thought it was funny because it was a utility van, but didn't have any signage on it. She also found it odd that the windows were partly rolled down, but no one was in it.

"Like she says, no one leaves their van unlocked around there," Julio said, giving Pete a piece of paper with the woman's information. "She thought someone was in the van. Maybe hiding."

Almost everyone else reported sightings that were too vague or would only be useful if we already had a suspect. A lot of witness testimony falls into the latter category. Someone saying they saw a blue sedan in the neighborhood doesn't help you when there are thousands of cars that match the description, but when you have a suspect who drives a blue sedan, you can go back to that witness and have them pull the car, and possibly the suspect, out of a lineup.

My phone rang with a call from the hospital. I listened, then hung up and told everyone, "Ray, our only real witness, just died."

On that depressing note, Pete gathered up all the reports and we called it a day. Pete and I made plans to meet at the office on Monday morning before driving to the autopsy. We were both looking forward to the opportunity to confer with Tolland.

A call from Dad meant stopping by his place on the way home to brief him.

"I see now why you didn't want me to quit the department," I said as I tried, unsuccessfully, to push Mauser's large butt off of my lap. "You just like having an investigator that you can ask to come by your house and give you a briefing whenever you want." I was only half kidding.

"Nonsense, I do that with all of my deputies," he said.

Not like you do with me, I thought as I filled him in on the results of the neighborhood canvassing.

"Typical."

"We're meeting with Tolland tomorrow after the autopsy."

"I'll be interested to see if Darzi finds anything that the earlier autopsies missed."

"Tolland forwarded all of the original reports to Dr. Darzi so he could compare them. He's already compared them with the first victim in the latest series and he's also looked at Tonya's X-rays to compare the blunt force trauma."

Mauser thought I was ignoring him and turned around, attempting to lick my face. It's not easy to have a serious conversation while warding off the attention of an animal that's the size of a black bear.

"Mauser, come on," Dad said, to no effect.

"I just wish there was a motive to work with. He's apparently not a sexual predator."

"We never ruled that out completely. It's still possible there could be a sexual component to this. A number of serial killers don't actually rape their victims, but still derive sexual pleasure from the killing. Admittedly, without bite marks or any of the other tell-tale signs, it seems less likely," Dad mused.

"A cleaver doesn't even seem as symbolic as a knife."

"True, not that I buy too much of that Freudian stuff," Dad said, getting up and fixing a Kong for Mauser, which finally got him to leave me alone.

I told him our plan to expand the suspect list.

"It's going to be bittersweet if we catch the guy and find out that we made decisions during the earlier investigation that meant we never had a chance of catching him. Regrets. They drive me crazy."

I knew that Dad wasn't just talking about this investigation, but also some of the lost time with my mother. He'd always worked long hours. They were deeply in love, and she'd understood the demands of his career, but he'd told me once how much he regretted not spending more time with her. Maybe that was another reason I couldn't commit to a career with the department. If Cara and I did become more deeply involved with each other, I wouldn't want to feel the same remorse that Dad did now. There is a real conflict that can exist between a career as important as law enforcement and the time you have to spend with the ones you love. Or maybe it's more about balance than conflict. I wasn't sure I was strong enough to find that balance.

"I'm not happy with what you did," Dad said suddenly. I knew he was referring to last month's debacle. "But you've got to push through it. If you don't want to be a deputy for the rest of your life, fine. But come back and push through the humiliation now. You'll be a better person for it. If I hadn't been so mad at you, I wouldn't have accepted your resignation so easily."

"I've got to get going. I'll let you know how things go tomorrow," I said, standing up and cutting off any deep discussions of my recent failings.

As I drove home I felt a little guilty for leaving like that. The weather reflected my mood as a cold front brought lashing rain and winds. But solace was waiting for me at home—Cara and a big bowl of home-cooked chili. I tried not to think about anything else for a few hours.

CHAPTER SEVENTEEN

I was up and out the door early on Monday. I met up with Pete at the office, and we took a few minutes to get our act together before we went to the autopsy. We organized the information we'd gathered from Sunday's interviews so we could share it with Tolland; hopefully he'd have some to exchange.

I drove, leaving Pete with his hands free to text back and forth with his wife and daughters.

"Doesn't Sarah have a job?" I knew his wife worked at a graphics company in Tallahassee.

"Yeah," he said while making rapid motions with his thumbs on his phone. How he could text so fast with those chubby fingers was a mystery.

"Her boss doesn't mind her spending half the day texting with you?" I prodded.

"No. She does the work her boss asks her to and he doesn't micromanage her time. Or badger her like some busybody partner. Besides, I'm not texting my wife. I'm texting Kim. She's at home with the flu." Kim was his younger daughter. "Shouldn't you concentrate on the road instead of worrying about what I'm doing?" he pushed back good-naturedly.

"Fine. If your thumbs fall off, don't come crying to me."

We parked and headed for the morgue. Tolland was waiting for us at the front desk, looking tired but determined to finish the job.

"I figured I'd wait for you. No sense making Darzi cover the same ground twice," he said, shaking our hands. "Let's do this first and then we can go over our progress… or lack there of."

Dr. Darzi was walking around the corpse, making notes, when we came in. He'd told me once that one of the biggest mistakes a pathologist could make was not standing back and looking at the body. Sometimes it's the forest you need to see.

"Hello, hello," he said, giving us a slight wave. Dr. Darzi never shook hands. Of course, I could count on one hand the number of times I'd seen him when he wasn't wearing gloves. "I think you all have a problem."

"We knew that," I said.

"Yes, of course. But the problem is bigger than you think," Darzi told us. "I've been studying the earlier autopsies." He pointed to pictures and various autopsy reports that were laid out on a steel table next to Dawn's body.

We all moved closer as Darzi explained.

"The original murders varied a bit in the initial attack. With the first murder, Tara Dunaway, you see there were three blows to the head. The first blow was glancing, the second to the back of the skull causing her to go down to her knees. From the angle of the final blow, he was standing above her and brought the blunt object down on top of her head. On the second murder where we have two victims, the woman, Tiffany Falls, was killed outright by the first blow to the back of her head. Her male companion, Jim Merrell, suffered several blows—one to the side of his head from the front, one to his arm, a defensive wound, and the final blow to the top of the head. The next three victims all suffered one mortal head wound from behind. He had learned how to kill efficiently."

"So what are you driving at?" Pete asked. Darzi held up a finger.

"I'm getting there, my friend. While there was some variation in the method used to incapacitate the original victims, all of them received a number of cleaver blows to the back. Between ten and fifteen. And most importantly, they were all at roughly the same angle and the same depth. The murderer was standing, straddling the body and hacking down at the victims' backs."

Darzi pointed to Dawn's body, lying face down on the table. "Now we have the new series of crimes. The first victim in this group, Shawna Morton, was killed the same way as was this victim, and as he attempted to do to Tonya Williams. However, Morton received twenty-five chops to the back with a meat cleaver. Only two of them are close to the depth of the wounds on the original victims. All the rest are deeper and came from a variety of angles, as though he was in a frenzy. Now we come to the latest victim."

He waved his hands over Dawn like a magician presenting his assistant. We all looked at the poor woman's back. It had been hacked pretty severely, but I didn't think there were as many wounds as the pictures of the victim before her.

"Doesn't look like as many wounds," Tolland mused, stealing my thoughts.

"Not quite as many. But deep. Some of them cut into the bone. He was crazed as he hacked at her. I think he is becoming more intense. I'm not a profiler, but if I had to guess, I would say that he is in crisis. He's dealing with it through these murders."

"So there's going to be more," Tolland intoned gravely.

"And we probably won't have long to wait," Pete chimed in.

We watched most of the rest of the autopsy, but didn't learn much. We asked if there was a room nearby where we could meet while Dr. Darzi finished up with Dawn. His assistant showed us into Darzi's office, where the walls were covered with gruesome pictures from hundreds, if not thousands, of autopsies. The bookshelves were filled with volumes on delightful subjects ranging from insect larvae life cycles to lividity analysis.

"Hell, we should have gone to my office," Tolland said regretfully, looking around at the macabre decorations.

"On the bright side, there's room for all of us to sit. We just have to remove various body parts to get to the chairs," I said, picking up a model of a liver... or maybe it was a kidney.

Once seated and trying to focus on each other instead of the gruesome surroundings, Pete and I updated Tolland on everything we'd learned so far.

"I'm pushing the forensics," he told us. "We've secured the cooperation of the FBI, but there's some effort involved in coordinating with their office. I did get to talk with a man I respect. Some of their profilers aren't worth dick, but this guy is solid. He'll give you what he's got without making up crap."

"Was he able to shed any light on the killer?" I asked.

"Not exactly. But he did say that these killings suggest the killer is a narcissist. Told me I might want to double-check with the papers and television stations and make sure they haven't received any mail, emails or phone calls from someone purporting to be the killer. He thought the purpose of the hacking was like a signature. The killer derives his thrill from the hunt and the kill. Then he puts his mark on the victim so everyone knows it was him."

"Interesting, especially in light of what Dr. Darzi said. He started out just putting his signature on the killings, but now maybe the savagery is more important," Pete said.

"We've already looked through the old reports for someone who might be trying to get close to the investigation, but I hadn't thought of double-checking with the media," I said.

"There have been cases, like the Long Island Killer,

where he contacted relatives of the victims in order to taunt them and to brag. We received a couple false confessions and some tasteless practical jokes during the first series of killings. No doubt, some of that will start back up now that it's in the news again."

"We should have a new list of suspects to check in a couple of days," Pete told him.

"And I'll have gotten at least a preliminary report on the forensic evidence we've gathered from the two newest murders. I also have our people going over the material that was collected at the original murder scenes. There have been a lot of advances in forensic science since then."

"What about the victims?" Pete asked. "They don't look similar. Several have been African American, and the women look a little bit alike, but…"

"I think it's less about appearance and more about availability."

"They all lived or worked in the poorer sections of Adams County."

"And they were all young," I pointed out.

"True. That may point to availability again. Young people tend to stay out later at night. The killer probably waited until after ten to make his moves," Tolland suggested.

"We can estimate when and where most of them were abducted," Pete added.

"But Tonya's is the only attack that we know had a witness. Unfortunately, he passed away yesterday," I said.

We were all quiet for a minute. "The hard part is knowing the difference between what's important and what's not," Pete sighed.

"It's always that way. After the fact, a lot of things become obvious. Tougher to see all those clues when you're running the scent," Tolland said.

"And we have to keep from getting attached to any one idea because the mind loves to make patterns where there aren't any," I stated.

"Couldn't be more right. Best we keep some of our more

speculative thoughts to ourselves," Pete said.

"We collect and share evidence, but not theories. Sounds good." Tolland stood up and promised us an update from his team soon.

Before we left the hospital, Pete and I went up to see Tonya. They wouldn't let us into the ICU, but she was awake enough that she managed a slight wave toward us after a nurse told her we were there.

"What do you think?" I asked Pete during the drive back to Calhoun, mostly to keep him from texting the whole way.

"I think we're in the same position a lot of serial killer hunters find themselves in. We're looking for a killer whose only motive is the desire to kill. Most homicides are solved by connecting the victim to the killer by past association and discovering a motive for the murder, but I don't think that's going to work with this one. These days we're lucky to be able to match DNA evidence… Assuming our killer leaves some at the scene and assuming that his DNA is on file somewhere."

"We could try setting a trap," I joked darkly.

"And I can't think of a single case where a killer has been caught using a trap."

"Hmmm, me neither. Always works on TV. We don't have any DNA…"

"There's been plenty of DNA recovered from the murder scenes, there's just no way to prove that whoever left it is connected with the crime. It'll be useful when we have a suspect, but not now," Pete pointed out.

"Right. So, no useful DNA, no obvious connection between the victims, no motive, no witnesses…"

"Again, we might have a witness who saw the killer's truck or van in the area, but we can't be sure yet."

"But we do have several vehicle descriptions."

"From both these murders and the earlier murders."

"We should go through them all and cross-reference them with our suspects."

"At least it will keep us busy." Pete didn't sound thrilled

with the project.

Back at the office we agreed that Pete would go out and re-interview the witnesses that saw promising vehicles. I went to check-in with Shantel and her efforts to grow our suspect list.

I found her sitting at my old desk. I stood over her, watching as she went through names and criminal backgrounds, cross-checking them with current police reports and utility records.

"If I sit at my own desk, I get interrupted every five minutes with someone wanting me to answer questions or help with something."

"I understand. Not my desk anymore."

This caused her to stop and glare at me. "When are you going to admit that you're working here?"

"I'm sort of working here."

"You got a new job?"

"I'm looking."

"And how's that going?"

"I hear you. Are you having any luck?" I asked, changing the subject.

She pulled up an Excel spreadsheet that had twenty-two names on it. "It's slow work. I've got a couple that look promising and another dozen that are pretty iffy... then a few in between. I'm probably missing a bunch who have sealed juvenile records."

"Nothing you can do about that. If he's in there, we'll just have to hope we come up with a witness or informant. Pete and I looked in on Tonya."

"She's doing better. Got a lot of memory loss and real bad headaches, but thank the good Lord she's alive. I still get chills thinking about what could have happened." Shantel locked eyes with me. "You found her. Saved her. That's why I'm not letting you quit."

An uncomfortable silence followed.

"I'll take the names you've got now and follow up on them," I said, looking for an escape.

Shantel printed them out and went over the details. I agreed that two in particular looked like real nasty characters. The good thing about people who are as bad as these two is that they usually have very short lives or, if they survive, they become permanent residents of the Florida State Prison at Raiford or some other quality government-run housing. Unfortunately, these guys had managed to reach the ripe old age of forty and forty-two, respectively, and had spent a surprising amount of time on the loose. Both had just missed being picked up in the original investigation because they were considered too young.

I decided to shoot from the hip and hit the best suspects first. Not that we weren't going to have to go through the whole list, but I wanted my dessert first. Besides, maybe my insightful questioning would cause one of them to throw up his hands and shout: *I did it!* Hey, a man can dream.

CHAPTER EIGHTEEN

I picked the younger guy first. He wasn't hard to find. He was serving six months' probation and his probation officer was happy to share that he worked on the loading dock of the AmMex trucking company.

When I walked up to the dispatcher, she glared up at me. "Eddie doesn't work here anymore," she barked.

"I'm looking for another one of your sterling employees, Rake Gunther." I had to admit that the poor guy was doomed to be a career criminal with a name like that.

"You know we're doing a good thing by giving guys a second chance, right? You all should just leave them alone." She kept those ice-cold eyes focused on me, then said, "He's in the back. I'll call him up."

I had an urge to tell her some of the things that this guy had done. That might have changed her mind about how much she wanted to defend him. But she did have a point. Ex-cons need jobs, and if AmMex wanted to employ them, who was I to stir the pot? Of course, it did make me wonder what AmMex was up to. I'd been a bit surprised when they weren't caught up in the DEA bust last month.

Rake came out of the back looking like the ex-con he was. He kept his angry eyes looking everywhere but at me.

He was a little shorter than my six feet even, with a receding dirty blond hairline. Around his arm was the obligatory barbed wire tattoo. Another tattoo was peeking up out of his shirt collar, but I couldn't tell what it was supposed to be. A goatee and mustache finished off his crime-life look.

"Yeah?" he said when he got close enough for us to talk.

I looked over at the dispatcher, who was obviously trying to listen to our conversation. "Let's step outside," I said.

"What do you think I did?" he asked as soon as we were out of the building.

"I don't know. Probably something criminal. But I'm here to figure out if you were involved in a very specific crime. If I can eliminate you as a suspect, I'll be on my way and you can get back to work."

"Sure." He didn't believe for a minute that I'd leave him alone if he answered my questions. Luckily, being on probation, he didn't really have a choice.

"Where were you last Saturday?" I asked.

"I don't know," he grumbled.

"Try harder," I suggested.

He sighed and looked back toward the door. "Okay, I don't know, maybe with some guys." He said it like he'd given me an answer.

"You aren't that stupid. You've been around the block a few times. You know what I need." I was getting a bit pissed.

"Yeah, well, how stupid are you? I don't want to tell you 'cause it would get me in trouble with my probation officer," he shot back. His angry eyes swept past mine, making contact for only a second.

"Do you really think I came out here to cause you trouble with your probation officer? If you've got an alibi for the time, I'll cut you loose. A solid alibi," I added. "And I don't need to tell you that *not* cooperating with me will definitely get you into trouble with your probation officer."

"All I was doing was partying with some friends. A buddy has a couple acres off of Sawgrass Road. We had a fire, some refreshments and some girls for entertainment. I was there all night." He looked past me, his body stiff and defiant. I understood his reluctance. There were at least a couple of parole violations right there.

"Names?" I asked, taking out a pad.

"Shit," Rake spat, but he knew that he didn't have a choice. A change came over him. His body relaxed and his face became an odd parody of a nice guy. "Look man, you sure you're not going to mess with me and my friends? We weren't doing anything. Just having some fun."

You see this all the time—an asshole reverting back to asking mommy and daddy to go easy on him. My skin was crawling.

"I told you the truth. Give me the names and, if everything checks out, we'll part ways." I didn't tell him that his fellow felons would have to do a pretty good tap-dance routine for me to believe them.

He gave me the full names and phone numbers of two of them and the nicknames of half a dozen others. I promised to go easy on them so they wouldn't feel like he'd ratted them out. Like I cared.

"What type of vehicle do you drive?" I asked. Shantel had found old DMV registration records for him, but nothing that was up to date.

"That's my truck over there." He pointed to an old black Chevy pickup at the back of the parking lot. "Actually, it's my brother's. He's letting me use it."

On my way out, I stopped and looked in the back of the truck. The bed was pretty clean, which seemed odd. It wasn't what I expected from Rake, but then it was his brother's truck.

I looked at the address of my other prime suspect. Conveniently, his house was on the way to Sawgrass Road, so it would be easy for me to check him out first and then follow up on Rake's alibi.

Brad Thompson was one of the vast Thompson clan, but apparently not one of the better connected ones. I'd never heard his name associated with the group run by Daniel and Justin Thompson. That was a good thing. Any business with them right now while they were awaiting trial and the outcome of several DEA and FDLE investigations would have involved me having to jump through all sorts of hoops.

Brad lived in a decent enough place, with a few toys in the front yard of the small vinyl-sided house. When I knocked on the door, a man wearing sweatpants and an FSU sweatshirt answered. He had a big smile that I thought couldn't be for me. His age was right, and he kind of looked like his mugshot, but I'd expected another variation on Rake.

"Brad Thompson?" I asked, expecting to be told that he had moved.

"That's me," he said, still sounding cheery. I showed him my badge. The smile faded, but didn't disappear all together. "Guess you want to come in," he said, backing out of the way.

The house was neat and clean with a slight odor of jasmine. He offered me a seat in the living room. "I know my past won't ever go away, but when it resurfaces it always comes as a kick in the gut."

"You seem to have made some changes in your life," I said. His record included two assaults, a laundry list of domestic abuse calls and an arson. That last was the one that got Shantel's and my attention.

"I found the right woman. Oddly, it was my wicked past that brought her to me. God's mercy." He sounded sincere. "What can I do for you?"

"We've got a violent crime we're looking into, and I'm afraid that when we were going through the records, your name came up. If you can tell me where you were last Saturday night, maybe we can all move on."

This was one of the things that made being an investigator so difficult for me. I wanted Rake to be in trouble, but I was hoping that Brad was clean. Fighting those biases was difficult; easier when you recognized them, but still a challenge.

"Okay, last Saturday. I was at an AA meeting. Saturday is at the First Baptist Church. I don't skip Saturday nights. Just something about the day of the week is a real trigger for me. About a dozen people were there. I can give you my sponsor's name, or you can come by this Saturday. The same people are usually there."

"How late did the meeting last?"

"We get done about ten. Stand around and talk for a while, and then I always help fold chairs and clean up. I must have left about ten forty-five. Something like that." It sounded airtight, but I would have to follow up.

I stood and he held out his hand. We shook. Was I just being manipulated? Our killer was a psychopath, so he would be capable of putting on a show like this. *Check and double-check the alibi*, I told myself.

It was late afternoon and the weather had started to change. Last night's cold front had stalled, but now the wind was picking up and dark clouds were blowing in from the west. We were in for more rain and temperatures below freezing by tomorrow night. Winter in North Florida ran the gamut from intensely beautiful to how-can-it-be-so-damn-cold-in-Florida? I figured I had just enough time to run out to Sawgrass and check on Rake's alibi before the weather turned wet.

The area was a collection of old trailers and small neglected houses. Mixed in was the odd house that looked like someone had received a windfall of money and built an addition or two before the money ran out. I had dispatch look up the address of the fellow Rake had said hosted the party.

The house was a shack that didn't have the ambition to fall over. I've seen crack houses that looked more habitable. In front of the house were two pickup trucks and an old K car parked haphazardly in the overgrown yard. As soon as I got out of the car, I could smell wood smoke and hear loud music—something I'd classify as hillbilly acid rock. I skipped knocking on the front door and walked into the side yard.

Three guys and a girl were sitting on improvised chairs around an oil-drum fire pit. The pit was about one hundred feet from the house, which was good since the house looked like a single spark would have given the neighborhood an amazing bonfire and an evening of entertainment.

The group was laughing, drinking beer and smoking as I walked closer. When they noticed me, two of them flicked whatever they were smoking into the fire. All of them looked at me like I was a warden come to check on his prisoners.

"Gentlemen, ma'am," I said congenially, but loud enough to be heard over the music playing on a jerry-rigged speaker set with someone's phone plugged into it. When I was twenty feet away, I stopped to give them all time to adjust to my presence. There was uncomfortable shifting and exchanging of looks between them. I recognized one of the men from a disorderly conduct and possession charge when I was on patrol.

"This is private property," grumbled a big guy with a full beard and ball cap.

"I just want to chat with you all about a friend of yours," I said with a smile that was met with grim stares.

"We don't talk to cops." This was from the fellow I'd arrested.

"Talking to me might help out your friend," I informed them.

"You think we're stupid. You don't want to help any of us," Beard said. The third guy and the woman both kept their eyes on the ground. It was pretty obvious that they were the ones who were most afraid of getting into trouble.

"How about you two? Would you all like to talk a little so that I can go away, and we don't have any issues?" I directed this at the last man and woman. Neither responded, but they were looking very twitchy.

It was a tough crowd. I decided to take another tack. "I'm investigating the Swamp Hacker. That's the only criminal matter I care about today."

When I mentioned the Hacker, all four of them looked at me. Beard's eyes shifted as he thought about this. "You're really after that son of a bitch?" he said, more thinking out loud than asking a question.

"That's all."

"Guess we can answer a couple of questions," he allowed grudgingly and everyone, including me, relaxed. "Lil, turn the music off." Lil turned out to be the woman. She unplugged her phone and reflexively checked it for messages.

"I appreciate that. This looks like a regular thing. You all sitting out here," I said. "Were you out here last Saturday night?" Looks were exchanged as they tried to figure out where I was going with this.

"Yeah," Beard said.

"I'm Deputy Larry Macklin," I said.

The third guy grunted. "Name's Diesel." I didn't press him for a real name, or point out that I'd known a Rottweiler named Diesel.

"Who was here?"

There was more thinking and exchanging of looks.

"I don't care if anyone was breaking parole or breaking any other laws. I'm like a bloodhound on a track. Nothing is going to distract me from who I'm hunting," I reassured them.

"I was wasted. Lil, you're the only one who doesn't have shit for memory. Who all was here Saturday?" asked Disorderly Conduct.

Lil looked shocked to be in the spotlight. "I don't know." I was afraid that was all she was going to say, but then she went on to prove herself wrong. "I was here, you three, David, Tucker, Joelle... Mad Dog and Missy came by for a while." She stared up at the sky, which was getting darker as the clouds moved in and the sun dipped below the horizon.

The fire felt pretty good. Diesel added a few more pieces of wood to the flames. Some of the scrap wood they had set aside for fuel looked like it was pressure treated. I thought about warning them about burning it, but figured the brain cells they'd lose to the burning of chemically treated wood was the least of their health concerns.

I was just about ready to prod Lil again when she seemed to remember more people. "Oh, yeah, Rake was here, and Gator. There were a couple more that came and went. I don't know all of their names." She looked at me for the first time.

"How long were most people here?" I was trying to avoid asking about Rake in particular. If they knew who I was focusing on, they might lie.

"Most of them got here in the afternoon and were so shitfaced they couldn't go anywhere else," she said with a little smirk.

"Okay, who got here and stayed the whole time?"

"Diesel, me, Tucker, Joelle, Rake, Gator."

"They didn't go anywhere?"

"Hell, they were mostly still here in the morning."

"Didn't go get any drink, or food or other recreational substances?"

"Didn't need to. I told you, Mad Dog came by and brought…" Lil turned red. "Nothin'," she said in a not-so-clever attempt to cover up the fact that she'd almost admitted that Mad Dog brought drugs to the shindig.

"Rake was here from Saturday afternoon to Sunday?" I couldn't put off asking a direct question any longer.

They all looked up at me again. It didn't take them long to come to terms with the idea that Rake could be the person I was interested in.

"Yep," she said, sounding very sure.

"Rake," Diesel said, shaking his head. "He can be mean as a snake, but he doesn't have the attention span to stalk and kill people."

It's always good to get an expert's opinion, I thought. Aloud I said, "I appreciate your help." I meant it and was pretty sure Diesel was right. Being a bastard didn't equate to being a murderer. "I might have to come back and talk with you all again." I turned to go.

"I thought he was going to ask about that creepy-ass van," I heard the woman say. It took me a couple steps before it registered.

I turned around. "What van?" I asked, walking back toward them.

"Now you've done it. He was almost gone," Beard said to her. She looked at him, trying to tell if he was kidding her or not.

"You thought I was going to ask about a van?" I prodded her.

Again she looked at Beard before answering. He must have given her a sign to go ahead, as she eventually said, "Yeah, I seen it a couple times."

"What did it look like?"

Lil shrugged. "It was white, or at least light. Could have been silver or something. I only saw it at night."

"Why did you think it was creepy?"

More shrugging. "It just, like, hung around. Never saw a driver. But it was weird. I came out of the house and saw it once. Saw it again when I was parked with a guy. Maybe again by the In and Out."

The In and Out was one of three liquor stores in the county.

"What kind of van was it?" I asked. She gave me a confused look. "Was it a family van or a work van? Big or small?"

"Like big… Kinda work type."

"Did it have windows down the sides?"

"No. I know 'cause I tried to see if someone was in it."

"Any writing on it? Maybe the name of a business?"

"No. I don't think so. I looked at it real close," she finished. I figured I wasn't going to get too much more out of her. The information was interesting, but not very useful. I might be able to get more out of her by showing her pictures, if I had any. Maybe later.

"Thanks. We might need to talk to you again." I got her

phone number.

One good part about being a reserve deputy—I didn't have to go back by the office and deal with any other cases. As I drove through Calhoun on my way home, I kept seeing white vans. Every plumber, electrician and AC contractor must have owned one. Many of them had writing on the sides, but some just had magnetic signs that could be easily removed. Why couldn't Lil have said she saw a DeLorean or a Tesla lurking in the neighborhood?

CHAPTER NINETEEN

Tuesday dawned cold and damp. Before I left the house, Pete texted me to meet him at Winston's Grill.

He was sitting in the back with a couple of empty plates laid out before him as he waved and spoke to various people coming and going. Most asked him how the hunt for the Hacker was going. Pete smiled and said we were making progress.

"So how *is* the hunt going?" I asked him when I sat down.

He leaned forward and spoke softly enough that only I could hear. "Unless you have a smoking gun, I'd say like crap." He smiled grimly and leaned back.

"If our killer is truly coming unraveled, we might not have much time," I said. Mary poured me some coffee and I put a couple packs of sugar in it.

"I'm well aware of that, Little Miss Sunshine." He said it lightly, but I could tell there was an edge to his mood. "You know, my daughters are only a few years away from being in his preferred age range. And when I think…" He shook his head. "Let's just say I don't want to think about that."

"We'll get him," I said, trying to sound more optimistic than I actually was.

"Your dad was a damn fine detective. I admire him. I've had reason over the years to go through some of his old cases and they're tight. Some of the most thorough I've ever seen. And Tolland is almost a legend."

"What's your point?"

"The point is that if this guy outfoxed both of them, then we might be in for a challenge that we can't meet."

"Which brings me back to what I said earlier. This guy is probably in meltdown. We might have been in over our heads when he was at the top of his game, but as he goes wild, he's going to get sloppy."

"That's a grim thought. The idea that we're lucky because he's been switched to berserker mode."

"It is what it is," I said. I filled him in on my interviews from yesterday. "What are your thoughts on the van?"

"Like you said, it's a long shot without more information. But on the other hand, it gives us something else to work with. I wonder if Tonya noticed a van before the attack?"

"Could have been days, even."

"If he was stalking her."

I called Shantel to check-in on Tonya. She was doing much better and had even been released from the ICU. Her memory was sketchy for the time around the attack, but the doctors were very encouraged. Shantel was going over to see her at noon.

Pete and I tried to think of the best way to work on the only lead we had. "How many white minivans have you ever seen?" Pete asked.

"Good question. Not that many."

"So let's assume it's a work van. Or at least it started life as a work van."

"That doesn't narrow the field much. Churches use them, just about every business that has to move inventory, as well as every electrician, plumber and carpenter."

"The law enforcement officer's lot is not an easy one," Pete joked. "We can reach out and bring in more deputies to help with some of the footwork."

"In a county our size… there are probably about a hundred white- or light-colored vans, and maybe another fifty that come into the county on a regular basis."

"You hit on something I've been thinking about. The killer might be someone who visits the county and drops the bodies off in the swamps on his way home to Leon."

"Another plausible theory. Great," I said sarcastically.

During our conversation, half a dozen folks came over and chatted with Pete and me. It was pretty obvious that most of them were interested in any news about the Hacker. I looked at each one and wondered if they might be the killer trying to find out if we were on his trail. Which was silly—most of them could be easily eliminated. Too old. Too female. Too unlikely.

Mary brought Pete's check. No check for me, as coffee was always on the house for law enforcement officers at Winston's.

"Your dad doing okay?" Pete asked the somewhat harried Mary.

"Not feeling well today, so I'm having to keep running."

"Sorry to hear that," Pete said sincerely. He took a deep interest in the health of Winston's Grill. It was the hub of his information network.

"He'll be fine. I'll tell him you asked about him."

At the office, Pete and I took over the main conference room and started going through motor vehicle records, making hard copies of anything we found on white- or light-colored vans registered to people or businesses in the county.

An hour into it, I realized two problems. "Damn, there are two groups we could be missing."

"What?" Pete said, looking up from his laptop.

"First, the van could have been painted since it was purchased and, second, if it's owned by a business, the business might or might not list this county as their primary address. Mill's Lumber and Supply has a dozen stores in the area. I think their main store is in Gadsden County."

"Good point. We'll just have to take care of these first, and if we don't come up with anything, we'll move on to other possibilities."

After three hours my eyes were dry and out of focus. "I've got fifteen vans."

"Twenty-one," Pete said, holding up his yellow legal pad.

I looked outside. The sun had come out, making the outdoors look inviting.

"Why don't we follow up on these and see where we are—" My phone went off with a call from Dad. "Hold that thought," I told Pete, who was chuckling at the new ringtone.

After the usual greetings, Dad asked me if I was busy. Alarm bells went off in my head—he usually only asked me that when he needed someone to look after his pet battleship.

"That depends," I told him. "Does this in any way involve Mauser?"

"Hear me out. Mauser is a part of this, but you'll be doing your job too. Shantel told me that Tonya would love to have a visit with Mauser. She met him at that church picnic a couple months ago and, well, Shantel thinks it might cheer her up."

"You're going to take Mauser into the hospital?" I asked incredulously. I'd met a few all-star therapy dogs over the years. Mauser was definitely not cut out for it. He had the ego, but he lacked the energy or the discipline.

"Not in the hospital. They've got their own therapy organization and rules, blah, blah, blah. But they did agree to let her see him outside in a little courtyard in the back of the hospital."

"Okay…" Reluctantly, I knew that this would give us an opportunity to speak with Tonya and maybe, hopefully, get some details that might help us if, by some miracle, she had any details to give us.

"Shantel said that Tonya would be willing to talk about the attack. Her only condition was that she get to see Mauser."

"It would be great if Pete and I could talk with her."

"Fine, I'll pick you up in half an hour."

"We'll just meet—"

"Nonsense, I'll be there in thirty," he said, hanging up.

I looked at the phone for a minute before turning to Pete. "If you've ever wanted to be stuck in a van with my dad and Mauser for a road trip to Tallahassee, your wish has been granted." I said it with a little more attitude than was justified, but Dad's manipulation of every situation to fit his plans was irksome, to say the least.

"We can interview Tonya?" Pete asked.

I filled him in on our new plans for the afternoon. He tried to convince me that we could just meet Dad at the hospital.

"Nope, I already tried that. Apparently Dad wants to have a captive audience." This case meant a lot to Dad, and he was doing a pretty good job of not looking over our shoulders, but I felt sure that he was looking forward to having us locked in the van with him so he could quiz us on our progress.

I called Tolland and brought him up to speed and invited him to be present when we talked to Tonya. Since we were going to be in his jurisdiction, I figured it was the right thing to do. He thanked me for calling, but said he'd leave it to us. "No sense in overwhelming her," he said.

When Dad's van pulled up, Mauser was bouncing up and down excitedly in the space between the front bucket seats and the bench seat in the back. Dad had taken out the middle row of seats to give the leviathan room. Reluctantly, I let Pete have shotgun. His three-hundred-pound frame was not built to crawl into the back of the van.

Mauser's glee at having me as a guest in the back with

him was painful, quite literally painful. First he jumped up and down, slamming my jaw with his blocky head as he tried to climb into my lap. Failing that, he turned around and sat on my knee, grinding his butt bone into my thigh.

I could tell that Pete and Dad were talking, but I was too far away and Mauser's loud panting made it impossible for me to make out anything but the occasional word.

"…witness… van… weapon… Tonya… last victim…"

I was never so glad to get to Tallahassee in my life.

Dad called up to Tonya's room while we took Mauser for a bathroom break.

"What are the odds that she'll remember something?" I threw out to Pete and Dad.

"With the head injury and trauma she received, probably slim to none," Pete said. "But you never know, and at this point anything would be a help. I think we should focus on the day or two leading up to the attack. She might remember seeing a strange vehicle or a person hanging around."

"I had a case a couple of years after I started—a hit-and-run where the victim was knocked unconscious. I interviewed him five or six times, and it was six months after the first interview that he remembered enough to help us find the car. We were lucky," Dad remembered.

"The doctor told Shantel that it could take up to two years for Tonya to complete the recovery process," I said solemnly.

It took us a few minutes to get back to the courtyard, mostly because everyone who came within sight of Mauser had to come over and ask how much he ate and if we had a saddle for him. Being the attention hog that he was, Mauser had to be dragged away from every new friend.

When we finally got to the courtyard we saw Tonya sitting in a wheelchair, her head bandaged and flanked by Shantel on one side and the largest woman I'd ever seen on the other. I remembered the big guy who was the nurse up in the ICU. *Where does the hospital get these people?* I wondered.

Mauser seemed to recognize Tonya. His whole body

149

began to wag, and it was all I could do to hold onto my end of the leash. He dragged me over to Tonya, whose face lit up in a smile.

The goliath standing next to Tonya frowned at Mauser and at the three of us.

"Let's be clear. My patient is still in a fragile state. I will call a halt to this when I think that she needs to rest." The woman, who would have been perfectly cast as the commandant of a Russian gulag, gave us all a stern glare.

For a few minutes everyone let Mauser give Tonya a proper monster dog greeting, with all of the slobber and head-bumps that entailed. He did take a second to greet Shantel, who he saw pretty regularly at the office. At one point he looked at the six-foot-plus nurse and seemed to consider introducing himself to her, but thought better of it.

Tonya returned the greeting with baby talk and ear rubs until Dad said, "Tonya, we'd like to ask you a few questions."

"She had a horrible headache yesterday," Shantel said with concern.

"I'm doing pretty good today," Tonya said, reaching up and touching Shantel's hand that rested on her shoulder. "I'll answer any questions I can, but my memory's still pretty messed up." She rubbed Mauser's ears as he leaned into her, then she looked up at me. "Auntie says you saved my life."

"She's known for exaggerating," I said, trying not to let my head swell. Though I did feel like I'd taken one step toward redeeming myself for the stupid mistakes I'd made last month. "We wanted to ask a few questions about the days prior the attack."

Pete lowered his bulk down beside Tonya, kneeling next to her wheelchair so that he was on eye level with her.

"We think it's possible that the person who attacked you might have followed you for a couple of days prior to the attack. So try and think back. Do you remember seeing anyone who seemed odd or out of place? Maybe someone you saw a couple of times?" Pete asked.

Her brow furrowed as she concentrated. "I don't know. It's kind of a blur."

"Try and remember what you were doing in the days leading up to the attack," I prodded and felt the Amazon glowering at me.

"I was looking for work. I picked up applications at a bunch of places, so I was driving all over town. I really need to find work in Calhoun. My car's a piece of sh... junk."

She recited a number of places that included just about every store and restaurant in town. "I even applied at Express Burgers. The manager was a jerk and the pay sucks, but it would have saved me that drive."

"Did the manager do anything in particular that upset you?" I asked.

"No, he just didn't act like he gave a damn whether I applied or not. You know, acted like it was a big deal giving me the application."

"Was anyone particularly nice to you?"

"Mary and her dad at Winston's, but I thought I might have an in there. I knew Mary from softball. She came out and helped coach the team before I graduated. And the woman who runs the Donut Hole. Betsy, or something like that. She said she had a hard time finding help that wanted to come in at four in the morning. Everybody else I talked to was, like, whatever."

Tonya leaned back in her wheelchair, looking tired. The golem shifted and I thought she was going to end the session. "Can you remember anything from the night of the attack?" I asked quickly.

Before she could answer, Mauser muscled his way back up to Tonya's wheelchair. She started rubbing his head as he nuzzled her leg. I could see her relax, and she began to speak almost absent-mindedly as her focus remained on Mauser.

"I just have... like, feelings. It was dark. A little scary maybe. I smelled something. Something familiar. And then nothing. I don't remember anything else until I woke up here." The last part I thought was a blessing.

"A smell?"

"I can't remember what it was. It's just like I thought… that's familiar, and then nothing. The man who… found me. What… why?" I could tell that she was struggling emotionally to deal with her captor.

"He's passed away," Pete told her.

"Yeah, Auntie told me that. But… Why? Why did he, you know, keep me? Auntie said that he was crazy."

"I think that's true. Or that alcohol had eaten up most of his brain. I don't think he meant you any harm. In fact, he probably thought that he was helping you."

She looked up at me and nodded. "I guess I brought him a bunch of trouble," Tonya said and Shantel squeezed her shoulder.

"Now don't you be thinking like that. He wasn't no saint. Just a dirty old man. Didn't mean no harm, but a dirty old man just the same," Shantel told her forcefully.

Tonya looked tired and Mauser's attention was beginning to wander.

"We probably ought to let her rest," Dad said.

"Took the words right out of my mouth," the mountain said. She reached down and unlocked the brakes on the wheelchair.

"Thank you for bringing Mauser," Tonya told Dad.

"So did we learn anything?" I asked as we walked back to the van. Mauser answered by lifting his leg on a spindly tree planted on a parking lot island.

"Not much. We do have this list." Pete held up his notebook where he'd written the names of the businesses she'd visited in her search for a job.

"Unfortunately, that includes most of the places in town. I doubt it's going to narrow things down much. Maybe if we compare it to places where Shawna and Dawn were known to visit during their last days."

"Don't forget the old cases," Dad said. "We gathered a lot of information on those victim's last days. Best we could."

"Good point. I'll get the list to Tolland so he can check it with the old cases," I told Dad. When I saw the look on his face, I realized what he'd really wanted. "Of course, it wouldn't hurt if you'd go back through the files too. I know you're busy…"

"No, I wouldn't mind. I might spot something," Dad jumped in. I smiled to myself. He knew that as sheriff he should stay above the investigation, but the failure to catch the killer years ago was still eating at him.

CHAPTER TWENTY

"I'll buy you all dinner," Dad said as we climbed into the van. I figured we were in store for the Dairy Queen drive-thru and my jaw dropped when he piped up with, "We can go to Bon Temps." I was shocked because Bon Temps was a nice restaurant with an upscale menu, while Dad was cheap with a palate that ran to roadside barbecue.

"What did we do to deserve that?" I asked, a little too sarcastically, and he answered in kind.

"Nothing. But they have outdoor seating so Mauser can sit with us and Genie is the manager."

"Genie?" The name sounded familiar, but…

"You remember Genie Anderson. She used to babysit you," Dad told me as we pulled into traffic.

"Oh, yeah. She had a kid that was about my age. But there was something wrong with him."

"There's nothing wrong with him. He has Down Syndrome. They moved into Tallahassee to be nearer to schools that could help him. Guess they moved when you were about nine."

"Timmy, or Tommy?" I tried to remember his name.

"Jimmy," Dad told me.

"I didn't know you kept up with her."

"I ran into her about a year back," Dad said without elaborating. Stuck in the back of the van and not easily able to keep up the conversation, I just let it drop.

After half the people sitting outside the restaurant, and a good part of the wait staff, had come over to greet and pet Mauser, and we'd finally placed our order, Genie came to our table. She was younger than I thought she would be, about five years younger than Dad. She must have had her son at a very early age. She had brown hair done up in a fancy French braid and her dress was simple and complemented her full figure. Only the lines around her eyes and some gray in her hair spoke to her age.

"Ted Macklin, what are you doing here?" she asked while petting Mauser, who assumed that everyone who came to the table wanted to rub his ears and make cooing sounds to him.

"We had some business at the hospital. This is Deputy Pete Henley." He introduced Pete, who awkwardly got out of the small metal chair and put his hand out.

"Just Pete," he said, acting very chivalrous as he gently shook her hand.

"And you remember Larry," Dad said as I stood up.

Genie turned and squinted her eyes at me. "Little Larry. Wow. You have grown. You were knee-high to a grasshopper last time I saw you. You work with your dad now?" she asked, making me feel like I was eight years old again.

"I'm a reserve deputy right now," I said simply.

"Oh, I heard... Well, never mind." She let it hang, making me wonder how much Dad had told her. And when?

She continued to pet Mauser and make over him. I looked at Dad and his face was all wrong. Sort of mushy and his mouth was doing something funny. Then I realized that he was smiling, really smiling. I mean, he smiles regularly enough, but it's usually just with a little lift to the corners of his mouth. But now, watching Genie, he was smiling like a deranged circus clown.

I looked over at Pete to see if he had noticed what was going on, but he had his head down, staring at his phone and swiftly texting.

Finally Genie smiled at all of us and left, saying that she needed to go back inside and keep an eye on things. But for one second, maybe two, I saw her and Dad meet each other's eyes. Just before it actually made me throw up, they broke it off. I spent the rest of the evening wondering about what I'd just seen. Dad flirting? I'd never seen him like that. When he was out meeting and greeting folks as their sheriff, he was always polite and a little country, but never flirtatious with the women. Never. As far as I knew, he'd never even gone on a date with anyone local.

The winter sun had gone below the horizon by the time our meal arrived. The food was excellent and warmed me as the temperature dropped. Mauser wolfed down the rice and chicken that Dad had talked the cook into preparing for him.

Genie brought Dad's receipt and credit card back to the table for the waitress. Clearly, she wanted to say goodbye to Dad. I was cornered into getting a hug from her.

"I'm so glad I got to see you again," she told me.

"Same here," I said. She seemed nice enough, but the effect she had on my dad weirded me out. I suspected that he'd had a fling now and then when he was at a seminar or law enforcement conference, but he'd always been discreet, for which I was very grateful.

It was completely dark by the time we all climbed back into the van. After a call to Cara and agreeing to meet her for dinner at her place tomorrow night, I settled back to digest my meal. Dad turned on the dispatch radio that was on the console as we got closer to the Adams County line.

Mauser and I were nodding off in the back of the van as Pete texted and Dad concentrated on driving. We had just crossed into the county when the radio started squawking out calls to patrol cars and, at almost the same instant, Dad's phone rang.

I opened my eyes and saw Dad hesitate to answer the phone. He wanted to concentrate on the calls on the radio, but the phone eventually won out. I couldn't make out what he was saying, but I saw Pete's head swivel to look at him. The van began to accelerate as Dad dropped the phone on the console and picked up the radio. Something was up and I was frustratingly out of earshot. Dad was shouting something into the radio. "Now... Where... I'm ten minutes away... On..."

The van continued to accelerate. We were on a divided highway and we began to overtake other cars. Dad didn't have any emergency lights or a siren in the old van, so the other drivers must have thought that a maniac was plowing down the roads that night.

I had to find out what was going on, so I got on my hands and knees and crawled up to the divide between the front bucket seats. "What's up?"

"A guy going home from work reported seeing a van down a dirt road. The van drove off, but the man was suspicious so he went and looked around where the van was parked. There was a body. He called it in maybe fifteen minutes ago. Just on our side of the line," Dad said, keeping his eyes straight ahead as he tried to focus on the dark road and the taillights and headlights of other cars.

"If we take County Road 280, we'll be heading toward the location," Pete said, looking at the map on his phone.

"Get on the radio and have dispatch vector some deputies in from different directions. Make sure that they are all aware that any van or suspicious vehicle should be stopped," Dad told Pete. To me he said, "Get on the phone to Tolland and have Leon County come in from their side. And see if they can get their helicopter over here." Dad was hunched over the wheel now, peering into the darkness.

I had to sit back on my haunches to use the phone as the van rocked a bit as it sped down the road. Mauser had picked up on the excitement and was bumping into me as I tried to dial Tolland's number. At one point I lost my balance and thudded against the door.

I managed to get the word out to Tolland. He sounded giddy with excitement, which was as out of character as my father smiling. He assured me that help was on the way. I hung up, wedged myself between the front seats again and told Dad and Pete that Tolland was sending reinforcements.

"Turn coming up! You take a left," Pete told Dad. "Three hundred yards... two..."

"Hold on to Mauser!" Dad shouted at me.

I looked at Mauser, who looked at me. His legs were spread wide and the whites of his eyes were showing. He was still wearing his harness and I reached out and took it in both hands, wondering who was going to steady who.

"Here!" Pete shouted over the radio that was crackling with deputies reporting in and dispatch moving them into place.

The van veered onto a narrow country road. Mauser and I managed to keep from rolling over, but it was a near thing.

"We're five miles out," Pete said.

I was back between the seats and peering out at the darkness that was suddenly pierced by the oncoming lights of another vehicle. Various dirt roads and private driveways whizzed by outside. I glanced at the glowing orange speedometer. We were barreling down the road at seventy miles an hour. This road was safe at fifty—in the daylight.

The lights coming toward us approached rapidly before turning right less than a hundred yards in front of us. In a flash we all saw that it was a light-colored panel van, but we couldn't make out any details.

Dad's reaction time was worthy of a much younger man. I swear I could smell the burning rubber as he slammed on the brakes. I just had time to grab Mauser and keep him from crashing into the door, but by doing so I sacrificed my own balance and hit the back of Pete's seat, hard.

Mauser smartly lowered himself to the floor of the van. I got up on my hands and knees again as we slowed down.

Dad hadn't been able to make the turn, so he had to make a U-turn on the narrow road, which had almost no shoulder. With a lot of cursing, he managed to get turned around faster than I think I could have done with that clunky minivan. Back we went and then made a quick right-hand turn onto the dirt road where the van had disappeared.

As soon as we had straightened out, Dad dropped his foot down on the accelerator and the engine churned and grumbled as we sped up. The dirt road hadn't been graded in a while and the van bounced and thumped as we sped through the night in search of the van.

Pete used the radio to notify dispatch that we had sighted the van. Our dispatcher had handed us over to the Leon County/Tallahassee joint dispatch so that they could coordinate all of us, including their air unit, in the search.

Poor Mauser whined and looked puzzled, wondering how our nice evening out at a restaurant had turned in to a nightmarish mad-cap dash over the backroads.

"Damn it," Dad said. "This road has a dozen different outlets."

"Plus the powerlines. Even a van could use the powerline access," Pete said. He was following the calls from the radio. "We don't have all the outlets covered yet."

Leon County's helicopter was still ten minutes away. Dad slowed down as we passed various crossroads and driveways. The recent rain meant that we couldn't rely on seeing a dust cloud from the other van as a clue to where it had turned.

"Damn it," Dad muttered again. We all looked at the darkness, knowing we'd lost the van but still hoping to see it. Now that he could stand up, Mauser joined me at the center console, trying to see what we were all looking at. It felt like a very dark episode of *Scooby-Doo*.

Fifteen minutes later everyone was in place. Dad and Tolland had established a five-mile perimeter around the spot where we'd seen the van. We had our deputies, Leon County's deputies, their helicopter and two state troopers who had been in the area.

Finally Dad suspended his own search for the van and took Pete and me to where the body was found. Marcus and Charlie Walton, another of our crime scene techs, and Deputy Julio Ortiz had already secured the scene and had it staked out with crime scene tape.

"I'm going to search every driveway, yard, garage and access road in the search area," Dad said after he'd dropped us off. "We're going to be at this all night and into the morning." He sounded grim and determined.

"Is there a chance?" I asked, standing next to the driver's side window.

"Honestly? I think he got away. If he was still in the search area, the helicopter probably would have picked up the van. But I'm not giving up. I'm going to take Mauser home and come back," he told me. Nodding toward the crime scene where Marcus had set up a generator and work lights, he said, "Maybe we'll get lucky. If he was interrupted, he might have made a mistake."

"If there's something here, we'll find it," I assured him.

He gave me a long stare. "I know you will. Get your head in." This last was directed at Mauser, who had his head sticking out the window of the sliding doors. The window started up and Mauser slowly withdrew back into the van. Dad put the van in gear and headed down the road.

Reluctantly, I walked over to the ditch that was illuminated by the work lights. Pete was standing on the edge of the road, looking down at a body that was clad in black slacks and a dress shirt. The victim was lying on her stomach and appeared to have been unceremoniously tossed from the road. Her back was a terrifying canvas of deep wounds. You couldn't even tell what color her shirt had been originally. Now all the shredded pieces were stained a dark brown.

I realized I had walked over to where the van had been parked and had a momentary panic attack. Were we walking on evidence?

"Has someone photographed the area up here?" I asked Marcus and Charlie.

"We did," Marcus said without looking up. "We had plenty of time while you all were driving up and down every dirt road in this part of the county."

"Did you get anything?" I asked, ignoring his jab.

"We got photos of tire tracks. Several different sets. Casts. Also, there were a couple of footprints, but they were scuffed out, so they won't be much good."

Pete looked up from his phone. "Dr. Darzi himself is on the way. He just texted me. His ETA is about ten minutes."

"Then I'm not going to touch the body," Marcus said. Normally they would look for ID, but if Darzi was almost there, the less hands on the body, the better.

"She looks like she's dressed for work," Pete said, peering down at the dark-skinned woman.

Looking down at her, I wondered if we had missed something in the earlier cases that could have helped us find the killer before her life was taken. I was gaining a new understanding of Dad's regrets over the Hacker case. Every victim was a milestone on our road to failure.

I watched Marcus as he used a flashlight to look in the shadows cast by the work lights. I knew that he'd be happier when Tonya was out of the hospital and Shantel stopped eating up her personal leave taking care of her. Shantel and Marcus were a team, and he seemed a bit lost having to work without her. Charlie was young and just out of college. We'd be lucky if he stayed with us more than a couple of years. He was always quick to suggest new techniques or technology that we could use, but he never seemed interested in mastering the fundamentals. He was only ten years younger than I was, but I found it hard to remember being that caught up in myself. Of course, that might just have been my own memory being kind to me.

"Found something!" Charlie yelled. He was five feet from the body and shining a flashlight down between some deadfall. I could see his breath in the glow of his light. "I'm going to need something to get it out."

"There's a pair of tongs in the van," Marcus said, looking

at me.

Charlie's find turned out to be a bottle cap. By the time we'd recovered it, Dr. Darzi had shown up with two assistants. On my way to the van with the evidence bag containing the bottle cap, I greeted him.

"Another body. This is not good." Darzi had a way with understatements.

"She's down there. Marcus waited for you. If you can find an ID, we can get to work notifying her family."

"If they've already taken pictures, I'll just need to check the temperature and take some measurements before we search the body."

I nodded and deposited the bottle cap in a large bin after I sealed the bag and labeled it. You could collect pounds and pounds of evidence, most of it unrelated and unimportant, but you had to treat all it like it could be a smoking gun until it was proven otherwise.

I walked up the road to where Julio was leaning on his car, staring at his phone and texting, or playing games, or browsing the Web or who knew what. When it came to social media, I was a bit of a Luddite.

"It's a sad, sad business," Julio said when I got within ten feet of the car. He put the phone down and stood up. "They haven't found the van." He nodded toward the radio on his shoulder that was crackling with calls as the coordinated search continued.

"Pete and I are going to need a ride," I said.

"No problem. Your dad's authorized overtime tonight so I can stay here as long as you need. A bunch of the guys came on duty to help with the search or to answer calls to cover for the deputies that are searching. You thirsty? Hungry?" he asked, walking to the back of his car. He opened the trunk where he had a small cooler. "My wife always packs me a cooler with drinks and snacks. Keeps me from spending money. We're saving for a house." He held out a bottle of water.

"Sure." I took it. "We'll probably be here for a couple

more hours."

"No problem." He got himself a water and an apple.

I made my way back to the glaring lights.

"Nothing," Pete said as I came up. "Hey, where's mine?" he asked good-naturedly, pointing at the bottle in my hand. I held the half-empty bottle out to him. He hesitated for a second before taking it and swigging most of it down. "Damn, I was hoping it was vodka," he joked, offering it back to me. I waved it off.

"Sorry, I can't find any ID. We might find something when we turn the body over, but I want to examine the back wounds before we do that. She does have a necklace and a ring that might help with identification," Darzi called up to us.

They removed the necklace and placed it in an evidence bag, handing it up to us. Pete showed it to me. It was gold, with the FAMU seal and the image of a rattlesnake. Florida A&M University was Tallahassee's second major state university, historically black with a solid reputation and a world-famous marching band.

"Worse, much worse," Darzi said. "More, deeper, from several angles." He was getting detailed pictures of the hack marks on her back. One of the assistants held the camera and the other a set of lights as Darzi probed the wounds. Finally he waved them away. The bigger of the two men carried the lights and camera up the bank and set them down before going back to the body. Gently, the three men turned the body over and placed it on a plastic sheet.

She must have been very pretty. Even in death you could see her striking bone structure and build. *The death of beauty.* Where had I heard that? Sadly, it seemed to fit this case.

We still couldn't find an ID. "She's what? Twenty-five? Twenty-eight?" I asked Darzi.

"Yes, about that," he said as he opened her mouth and reached in with his gloved hand, feeling around for anything that might be loose in her mouth. Much of this would be done again at the morgue, but things can happen in transport, and I've heard Darzi berate one of his assistants for not doing a thorough enough examination onsite.

"I really want to catch this son of a bitch," Pete said, surprising me with the anger in his words. Pete seldom used profanity and let his temper show even less. "I just think about my daughters in a couple of years. Going to school, finding jobs, looking toward the future and then some animal comes along and does this." Pete seemed older in that moment, and I was reminded of what it must be like to carry the responsibility of being a parent.

"What eats at my heart is that this guy is out walking around every day. We might pass him on the street or stand behind him in line at the grocery store," Pete said.

"Don't get philosophical after midnight. That only leads to drinking and depression," Darzi said without looking at us. "I think we can move the body now," he said to his assistants. The victim was carefully hauled out of the ditch and placed in the coroner's van for the trip to the hospital.

"Catch this guy," Darzi said as we shook hands. "My wife doesn't like me coming out in the cold in the middle of the night. I don't like it either."

"We appreciate—" Pete started to say, but Darzi waved it off.

"We are all just doing our jobs."

CHAPTER TWENTY-ONE

It was almost four in the morning when we walked back to Julio's car.

"They've called off the search. But I don't think your dad has gone home. I heard him on the radio a minute ago saying he was going to check out a couple more houses that were just outside the original search area," Julio told me.

"I'm not my father's keeper. I can't make him go home and get some sleep." I knew from growing up with him that, even if he went home, he probably wouldn't be able to sleep. Many nights I'd gotten up to discover him sitting in the living room with a glass of bourbon by his recliner, staring off into space, reliving his day and trying to catch bad guys in his head.

"You all mind riding in the back?" Julio asked us. On a good day, the laptop and gear in a patrol car made it a tight squeeze to get into the passenger seat, but his was even worse. Like a lot of deputies, he'd filled the seat up with his personal equipment. He even had an office organizer in the seat, stuffed with all sorts of odds and ends.

"Sure," I said.

"Actually... I hate to sit in the back," Pete said. With both of us looking at him, he went on. "Not because I'm fat.

I just hate being locked in the back."

I just stared at him, trying not to laugh.

"Don't look at me like that. I have nightmares about the six months I had to do at the jail when I started. I almost quit. I don't like being locked in. Sorry." As easygoing as Pete usually was, both Julio and I realized that if he was putting his foot down like this, he was serious. We pitched in to help Julio put his stuff in the trunk, but I couldn't resist giving Pete a hard time.

"Control freak much?" I asked.

"We all have our fears," Pete said defensively. "Rumor has it you're not a fan of heights."

He had me there. "Not a rumor. I hate cliffs, tall bridges, high buildings. There's a reason I live in a town in Florida without a single building more than two stories tall." I still had the occasional nightmare about a fall I'd taken off of a bridge back in December.

We'd already given dispatch a description of our victim so they could notify other law enforcement agencies. If anyone within a hundred miles reported a woman missing who matched our Jane Doe, hopefully we'd get a call. All we could do now was wait for her family or friends to notice. The morgue would take her fingerprints and DNA, but that would take a while to check. I was pretty sure we'd have a report before then. Our victim looked like someone who would be missed.

Ivy got tired of walking over my sleeping body about one o'clock and started meowing at me until I woke up. I'd filled up her bowl when I got home around four-thirty, and that had kept her mollified until afternoon, but she'd decided that if I was going to be home half the day then I should at least be spending it scratching her back or something else equally useful.

When I checked my phone, I had a texts from Pete and Cara. Pete's was only half an hour old. *Possible victim. Family contacted office. I'm going to check it out.* I called him.

"I'm on my way now. They live south of town," Pete said.

"You want to meet? I'll go with you."

"Sure, see you in the parking lot of Winston's."

"Give me half an hour."

"Take your time. I'll have lunch."

The text from Cara asked if we were still on for dinner that night. I texted her to call me when she had a break at the vet. She called as I was locking my front door.

"I know where you were last night. You okay?"

"So-so. I'm going to meet Pete, and we've got a possible lead on the parents of the victim. I guess the latest murder is all over town?"

"And online."

"I can't decide how I feel about Shantel dragging me into this."

"Hey, now. Tonya probably wouldn't be alive if you hadn't agreed to help," Cara chastised me.

"You're probably right," I agreed, trying to hold the phone, open the car door and get in the seat at the same time. "I just feel like I've been sucked into the vortex of my dad's unsolved case. And I'm not sure that I'm going to be any more successful than he was."

I had to juggle the phone a bit more when I got out to close and lock the gate leading back to my house. I'd tried to do that a little more these days. Better safe than sorry.

"I have faith in you," she told me and, as corny as it sounds, I found it comforting.

"I'll try not to let you down," I said lightly, a little embarrassed that it had felt so good to hear.

"Make sure you don't," she joked back. "When do you think you'll be done?" she asked and then quickly added, "I know you can't give me a guarantee."

"Let me meet with these folks and find out if we've identified our victim. I'll know better what my day is going to be like after that."

Pete was leaning against his car, a toothpick in his mouth, talking to one of the local hay farmers. Hank Parrish drove a truck that looked like it was a miracle it ever started and wore jeans that were just one wash from falling apart, but he owned several thousand acres of prime hay fields.

Pete pointed to me and Hank followed him over to my car.

"Mr. Parrish, how you doing today?"

"Getting ready for spring. How's your dad?"

"He's been better," I said as Pete got into the passenger side.

"Tell him I'll be around in a day or two. Might make him feel better," Hank said, lifting his arm in farewell and walking off.

"What was that about?" Pete asked.

"Mr. Parrish helped Dad with his last two campaigns for sheriff. I guess he's going to make a contribution to Dad's reelection. That will cheer him up a bit. Dad hates having to cold-call people for contributions, but these days it takes money to run any campaign."

"I know it doesn't help that Maxwell threw his hat into the ring," Pete said. Dad had been fuming about Charles Maxwell, Calhoun's chief of police, running against him ever since he found out.

"Exactly."

Pete gave me the directions and we headed to a community just south of Calhoun.

The house was set back off of the road on a slight rise. A well-kept yard of at least five acres framed the large modern structure. A flagpole with an American flag formed the centerpiece of the driveway.

The front door opened before we were out of the car and an anxious-looking woman in her mid-fifties, dressed professionally, stood with her hands nervously rubbing each other.

"What's happened? The officer wouldn't tell us anything, just that investigators would come and talk to us."

"Can we go inside?" I asked.

"Of course." She turned and we followed her into a house that was as immaculate inside as out. A tall straight-backed man with an ebony complexion stood waiting in the living room. He stepped forward and extended a hand.

"Martin Grey," he said, and Pete and I introduced ourselves in turn.

"I'm sorry, Alisha Grey," the woman said, her hands stopping their nervous massage long enough to shake hands.

Pete and I exchanged looks. We had both seen the section of the living room set up as an honor wall for our victim. Most of the awards didn't look like the kind they give just for participation. I saw large trophies for both golf and tennis, and behind them were pictures of their daughter draped with various medals.

"I'm afraid that we have some very bad news," was the lame platitude that came out of my mouth.

Mrs. Grey began to hyperventilate. "No, no, no," she said, shaking her head and sinking into a chair.

Pete had taken a picture of the necklace and, even though it seemed obvious that we had the right woman, he showed the picture to Mr. Grey.

"Do you recognize this necklace?"

"Where is she? Is she at the hospital?" he asked, desperate for us to give him a little hope.

"I'm afraid that we found this on a woman who was…" Pete could hardly bring himself to tell them. "Deceased."

Mr. Grey began to pace up and down the room. You cannot predict how people are going to react to such devastating, life-altering news, but most people fit into several categories. Mr. Grey was heading solidly for angry denial.

"What the hell are you saying? What bullshit is this? My daughter isn't some crack whore. You're crazy. You cops are all alike. Think that any black person is going to get shot down in a gang fight."

"Please, Mr. Grey, it isn't like that," Pete said as the man continued to pump himself up, the veins beginning to bulge in his neck.

"Don't tell me what it's like. You've made a big mistake. You need to go out there and find my daughter." He got into Pete's face and pointed outside.

I stepped forward, trying to take some of the heat off of Pete. "No one would be happier to find out that this is a mistake than we would. But I saw the body last night. There is a very strong resemblance to the woman in those pictures," I said, pointing to the honor wall of photos.

For just a moment, he followed my finger and saw his beautiful daughter smiling broadly in tennis outfits and golf shirts. Something got through to him.

"I want to see her," he stated. He was calmer, but you could see the waves of emotion that he was holding back.

"Of course. We can go right now." I couldn't blame him. His demand was reasonable and understandable, and I wasn't going to put up any road blocks. "We'll be glad to drive both of you to the… hospital."

"I'll drive." He turned to his wife and took her arm, gently helping her up off of the couch.

"We'll need to ask you some questions afterward," I told him.

"First, I want to see this person you think is my Jillian," he said flatly.

Pete and I went back out to the car while the Greys left through the garage. As the garage door lifted, I saw the Marines bumper sticker and tag frame on their car and understood a little more about Mr. Grey.

The visit to the morgue was horrible, as these experiences usually were. Her mother broke down completely, to the point that I thought a doctor was going to have to be called in for her. But Mr. Grey managed to lift her up off of the floor and, after talking gently to her, wiping her tears and holding her, he was able to get her back on her feet.

Pete and I led them to a small security office near the morgue where we could ask them questions. I hated having to press them for answers at a time like this, but we didn't have a choice.

"Where did Jillian work?" Pete started.

"Homegrown Foods in Tallahassee," Mr. Grey said. "She's the produce manager there. It's a big job. They only sell locally grown organic food, and her job is to make sure that the sellers aren't cheating. She'd even drive out and check the farms. She liked to say it isn't cheap, but it's real. I guess a lot of places claim to sell local food, but cheat or just out-and-out lie. She could have done anything. Jillian was *cum laude* from FAMU. I'd have gladly paid for her college, but she got a sports scholarship. Her degree was in nutrition." He finally stopped. You could physically feel the pride that he had in his daughter.

"Did she go to work yesterday?"

"Yes. I saw her leave around eight o'clock. That was the routine. She got up, exercised and then went to work."

"But she didn't come home?"

"I don't know. Neither one of us saw her after she left in the morning." He looked over at his wife, who was staring down at her hands that were clenched on top of the table. She hadn't spoken a word or acknowledged anyone else since we left the viewing room.

"Was that unusual?"

"No. She lived in the apartment above the garage. It has a separate door. We didn't realize anything was wrong until the owner of Homegrown Foods called us and asked if everything was okay. That's when I went and checked. Once I saw that her car wasn't there, I called you all." Mr. Grey said everything as if he was testifying in front of Congress. He'd pushed his emotions down and was letting his professional demeanor take over.

"Had she complained about anyone following her, or strange men hanging around the store?"

"Nothing. And she would have told one of us. When

Jillian was younger, we moved quite a bit and sometimes lived on military bases where there were a lot of young men. I made sure that she knew how to protect herself. I drilled into her the importance of situational awareness."

"So no phone calls or troublesome texts?"

"No. She seemed fine. Not worried about anything."

"But you didn't always see her for more than a hello in the morning, is that right?"

"On the weekend we almost always spent time together. I grill out every Sunday, and Jillian is always there unless she's out of town. Of course, the store is closed on Sunday."

"She loved the store." Her mother spoke for the first time. We all waited, but she didn't say anything else.

"And the owner was good to her. They'd talked about her becoming a partner," her dad continued.

"What about a boyfriend?" I didn't think that a boyfriend had killed her, but if she had one we'd need to talk with him. And there was always the very slight chance that this murder wasn't connected to the others. Though I didn't believe it for a minute...

"No. Jillian didn't spend much time with boys."

"Girlfriends?"

I saw Mr. Grey bristle at the question as though I'd suggested something improper. There are still some folks that feel that way.

"No. She wasn't like that. Look, I know it may seem odd that she wasn't hanging out with some boy, but she just didn't have the time. Jillian tried having boyfriends when she was in school, but she complained that they either distracted her from her training and studies, or they resented the fact that she spent so much time practicing and working on her classes."

"I asked her all the time when she was going to find a husband. And she always said, 'Momma, there's plenty of time for that.'" Mrs. Grey let the sadness of that statement hang in the air.

"Well, what about friends?"

"Like I said, we moved around a lot when I was a Marine. She made friends, and there's a few that she still keeps up with, but it's not like when you live in the same town all your life," he stated.

"She went out with the folks from her job sometimes. After they closed, they'd go to a restaurant or sometimes a bar," Mrs. Grey said.

Pete and I looked at each other. There wasn't much point in continuing to torture the couple. We'd have more questions, but for now the kindest thing we could do for them was to let them go home and grieve in private. We got their contact information and permission to search her apartment above the garage, but there wasn't much else we could do. It seemed clear that Jillian was an open person who lived for her work. There was always the possibility that she had some secret life that her family didn't know about, but I didn't think it likely.

We walked out with the Greys and, before parting, asked them not to go into her apartment until our crime scene techs had gone over it. Pete and I also vowed that we'd do everything in our power to catch her killer.

Mr. Grey had one more question to ask once his wife was in the car and out of earshot. "Is this connected to the Swamp Hacker murders?" he asked.

I had no choice but to tell him the truth, if for no other reason than that reporters would soon be all over the story, if they weren't already waiting for the Greys at home. "Yes. I know that's going to make it tougher on you and your wife. The reporters are going to be pretty aggressive."

"Tougher. I…" His eyes got moist and he just turned and got into his car.

The sun was shining and the air was crisp, but the weather didn't do much to improve our mood. Pete and I decided to stop by Homegrown Foods while we were in Tallahassee.

"Thoughts?" I asked Pete, who was looking out the window, too downhearted to text.

"I think everyone's right and the psycho is going psycho. But this one may be our break. The attack doesn't fit the pattern," he said.

"We haven't found the car. Maybe it does fit." I played devil's advocate, but I felt that he was right. Something was different about this one.

"She's not his normal victim. Jillian lived in an upscale house. Had a solid job. I can't see her hanging out in a bad neighborhood."

"Again, we haven't found her car."

"But she didn't have a boyfriend, certainly didn't seem like the type to be taking drugs, didn't have any relatives in the area."

"So her parents said." I held up my hand. "I believe them, but…" I let that linger. "Until we find the car… Maybe she was taking someone home or stopped at the wrong minute market."

"It's possible." He called dispatch on his phone and had them pull up Jillian's vehicle registration. "This is a priority. If anyone spots it, they are not to approach it and should call me or Macklin immediately." They must have asked if he was talking about me or Dad because he said, "Either."

"Call Tolland and tell him what's going on, ask him to put out the BOLO on the car too, and tell him he can meet us at Homegrown if he has the time." I'd talked to him when I was on the way to meet Pete, and I knew that he had also spoken to Dr. Darzi.

As horrified as we both were at this murder, we had to wonder if it would provide the break we were looking for.

"We'll need to talk to all of our suspects again," Pete stated.

"Yep, and find out if they have an alibi for last night." We had a precise point in time when we knew where the killer was. This gave us a tool that could be used to eliminate some of the suspects, and perhaps focus attention on others. Sadly, in serial murder cases, each additional murder is welcomed for the information it can provide.

CHAPTER TWENTY-TWO

We met Tolland outside of Homegrown Foods. We went in and talked with as many of Jillian's co-workers as we could. They all painted the same picture as her parents had of a woman who was dedicated to her job and to living a healthy life.

We met with the owner in his office. Derin Crane wasn't much older than me, maybe in his late thirties. He had a goatee and deep-set eyes that seemed much older than the rest of him.

"Jillian was much more than an employee to us. I started Homegrown five years ago and was struggling until she joined us in the second year," he said.

"She was your produce manager?"

"That was just part of her duties. I hired her because she knew what healthy food was. Just because it's called a tomato doesn't mean that it has any real nutritional value. She went to farms and saw how people grew the food. She would inspect the plants that the produce came from, and cut a piece of fruit or a vegetable open and examine it before she agreed to buy a farm's produce. And it didn't stop there. After she'd been working here a couple of months, she came to me and suggested changes in how the store was arranged that would make the produce last longer. Jillian was a genius. I know that sounds odd to say when you're talking about running a grocery store, but it's true. I really… I don't know how I'm going to replace her."

"She wasn't unhappy about anything? A customer maybe? Any of the other employees bothering her?" Pete asked.

"No. I would have done anything to make sure she was happy. I planned on making her a partner. We were just working out some of the financial details," Crane said, looking lost.

"Had anyone odd been hanging around the store lately?"

"No. We've had problems in the past with the homeless taking advantage of the good nature of our customers. And we've helped some of them. With others we've had to rely on the police to issue trespass warnings."

"No odd cars in the parking lot?"

"Nothing in the last couple of months. Again, in the past we've had cars that were abandoned here, or people who broke down and were begging money. We help those we can."

"What time did Jillian leave last night?" I asked.

"I don't know. I've been trying to remember. I think it was pretty early. She usually let John or someone close up for her. She… You have to understand what she did. I already told you that she found the best locally grown food in the Big Bend, and she saw that it was in good shape when it arrived. But beyond that, she'd see that it got to the restaurants that buy from us in good shape, and that the cooks and owners were happy with what they received."

"She worked directly with the restaurants?"

"Exactly, that's how she helped make us profitable. All of our customers were happy with the goods we provided and the professional attention that she gave them."

"Did she have any particular friends at work?"

"A funny question. She… had a professional relationship with everyone. Not that she wasn't friendly. Jillian even went out with all of us after closing sometimes. But she never quite crossed the line from colleague to friend. Even when we went out, she'd be one of the first in the group to make excuses and leave. She was the perfect workaholic."

Everything he said backed up what her co-workers had told us.

"Sometimes you just have to give up and believe what people are telling you," Pete sighed.

We went to a Mexican restaurant on North Monroe Street to talk.

"Nothing on her car yet?" Tolland asked.

"Not on our side of the line," I said

"Nothing on the van either," Pete said as he steadily made his way through the basket of chips on the table. "Your dad talked to the witness who reported seeing the van while we were still working the crime scene."

"That's news to me," I said, but I wasn't surprised.

"The guy didn't give him much more than was in the initial report." Pete stopped eating chips long enough to take out his phone and fiddle with it. "Here's your dad's report. The witness saw a man, described as large, maybe six foot, not fat, but solid, wearing jeans, a dark coat and hat, ball-cap style, come from behind the van, get in the driver's side and drive off. He said the van appeared to have its high beams on which kept him from getting a good look at the front of the van or the person driving. The witness stopped, found the body, blah, blah, blah."

"And we just saw a flash of a light-colored panel van," I told Tolland, who nodded.

"I'm willing to go with the assumption that it was the killer. And that killer is *our* killer, not a copycat. And if that's the case, then we know exactly where he was last night."

"And it gives us a way to eliminate suspects. Pete and I already talked about that."

"Plus it puts him in a light-colored van," Pete added.

"When we re-interview our suspects, there's two points we need to focus on. Do they have access to a van and do they have an alibi for last night?"

"They would also have had to have access to the van last night," Tolland pointed out.

"True. If it's a work van and they couldn't use it at night, that doesn't help us," Pete agreed.

"From here on out, we need to be very careful. We screw up, and our killer gets a heads-up and destroys evidence before we can get a warrant," Tolland said.

"And lawyers-up."

"Exactly. Also, when we question them, there should be two of us, if possible. If we catch them by surprise, they might make up an alibi or lie about the van, and it would help to have two of us to corroborate the statement," Tolland suggested.

"Agreed," I said and Pete nodded.

"I've got a couple of people on my team to help out over here. But I know you all are pretty short-handed. If you need some help, just let me know. I'd be glad to come over and lend a hand," Tolland offered.

"Must be nice working for a department with resources," Pete said, not meaning a word of it. I knew for a fact that he loved the freedom he got working for a small office.

Pete and I agreed that we needed to get onto the suspects as soon as possible. People's memories are bad enough, but with time they become worse, more malleable and eventually pretty much worthless. We'd try to talk to at least one this afternoon, take a break for dinner and then try a couple more in the evening. Weekday evenings were the best times to catch people at home.

I'd texted Cara and told her I'd be over for dinner, but wouldn't be able to stay long. Then Pete and I went directly to the first suspect on my list.

"Brad Thompson. Great. I take it this isn't one of the better Thompsons?" Pete asked.

"He's not bad. Seems to have got religion. AA. Living

clean. The whole routine."

"Okay, he goes to the top of my list," Pete joked.

Brad wasn't at home, but an elderly neighbor—as a deputy you just have to love nosey old folks—said he worked part time at the First Baptist Church. It was the largest church in Calhoun. Its sanctuary, pre-school, playground and parking lot took up a whole block of tax-free real estate in the middle of town. Due to its size, many people assumed that the Baptists were the first in the county, but the area had originally been settled by Presbyterians—Scotch-Irish who'd moved down from Georgia and the Carolinas in the 1830s and '40s.

We found Brad painting a door frame in the back of the church.

"Hello!" I yelled so he could hear me even with the earphones that he was wearing. Brad jumped and turned around, spilling some paint on his overalls.

"Sorry," I said sincerely.

"It's okay. I like to listen to music when I work." His tone was neutral. He wiped the brush off and set it on the edge of the can. "Figured I wasn't done with you all."

From where we stood, I could see a white church van parked near the building, but there was writing on the side of it. I was pretty sure that the van we saw didn't have any. Did the church have another van?

"Where were you last night?"

"At home with my wife."

"Do you ever drive the church van?"

"I have, once or twice, to get building supplies."

"Is that the only van they have?" I asked, pointing to the one I could see.

"No. There's an older one. In fact, I use the older one." He was answering every question with an open and honest expression. Brad struck me, as he had the first time, as a man at peace with himself. Of course, Ted Bundy probably would have too.

"Could we have a look at the other van?" Pete asked.

Brad led us around to a shed where a lawnmower and other equipment was stored. An older white van with faded lettering on the side was parked behind the shed. I tried to decide if the lettering would show up at night. Still, would you use a van with a name painted on the side to stalk, kill and get rid of people? I doubted it.

"Do you have access to any other vans?"

"No." I knew he didn't have a van registered in his name or his wife's name.

"Can we look inside?" I asked, pointing at the van.

"I guess. It's not mine, but I don't think the church has anything to hide. I'll go get the key."

Pete and I peered into the back windows as best we could and checked the tires to see how dirty they were.

"Van doesn't look like it's been driven on a dirt road recently."

"Hard to tell. But honestly, it doesn't look like it's been driven for a few days." Pete pointed out the leaves on the windshield.

The inside was clean, but not too clean. We thanked Brad and left.

"I'll talk to his wife, but I think we can put him on the back burner," Pete said, sounding tired. I dropped him off at his car and we agreed to meet back at the office at seven. We could get one or two more interviews done tonight. At this point it felt like any minute we might get lucky, but the truth was that it might take days, weeks or even months.

I picked up a pizza from a local chain and headed to Cara's. She opened the door with a smile, though it could have been just for the pizza.

"Smells good," she said and gave me a quick kiss that made me feel all soft inside. "What are you smiling about?" she asked.

"You… Us."

"Talk like that will get you everywhere. I baked some chocolate chip cookies yesterday. We can have them for dessert."

I avoided all the suggestive comments I could make about dessert. "Cookies and pizza. Makes me feel like I'm in college again. All that's missing is the beer."

"That can be arranged," Cara said, laughing.

"'Fraid not. I've got to go back out with Pete tonight."

"You're no fun," she joked, getting plates down from a cabinet while Alvin got under foot. I called him over and scratched his back, but all he wanted to do was smell me for signs of Ivy. He and Ivy definitely had a love/hate relationship.

"You're going to get yours, young man," she told Alvin. "I've got a raw bone in the freezer for him," she told me.

With our stomachs full and Alvin gnawing away happily at his bone, we leaned back on the couch. "How's it going?" Cara asked softly, taking my hand.

"It sounds horrible to say, but yesterday's murder is going to help. But telling her parents was enough to rip my heart out. The hell of it is, all the victims have been young and with a lifetime ahead of them. Some might have had better lives than others, but who's to judge? Everyone deserves their chance and these women didn't get their opportunity…" My voice trailed off and Cara squeezed my hand.

"One of my early worries was that this job would make you hard and unfeeling. Now I'm worried that you aren't hard enough." She smiled to let me know she was kidding. "I know you can handle it. Just remember that you don't have to go through it alone." I leaned into her and gave her a gentle kiss, drawing back before it became more.

"There is one more thing that's been bothering me," I started, knowing I was headed into dangerous territory. "These women… It's such a dangerous world. When I see people, young and innocent people, getting killed for no reason and then I think of you… I worry."

"That's sweet. But I'm okay. I leave my house, go to my job, come home…"

"I know. It's just that you're here alone…" I was still

tiptoeing around the subject.

"I've got Alvin. He even goes to work with me sometimes." She chuckled at the idea of the twenty-pound Pug defending her. "I know you see a lot of bad things. I watch the news. I hear people talking. I've even seen some bad things. But you have to remember who my parents are," Cara told me. Her words brought back memories of her strong Viking father and her sweet, though rather odd, mother.

"Yeah, but…"

"Oh…" She seemed to realize something. "What? Are you asking me to move in with you?"

"What? No! I mean, no. That would be… Something we'd need to talk about…" *How the hell did I get here?* I thought, more than a little panicked.

Cara laughed. "Don't worry, I'm not trying to crowd you, but then what *are* you thinking about?" She poked me in the ribs playfully.

"I was thinking it wouldn't be a bad idea if you had a gun," I said flatly, afraid of her response.

Her playful mood evaporated. "A gun?" she asked, with almost no inflexion in her voice and no clue to tell me if I had stepped on a landmine or not.

"I'd show you how to use it. Or better yet, I'd get Pete to show you. He teaches classes to civilians as well as law enforcement officers," I finished lamely.

"It might surprise you to know that I've shot a gun before," she said, still with almost no hint as to what she was thinking. "Dad taught me. You have to remember that he's an old-school, live-off-the-land sort of hippy. I can't say that I took to hunting, but he taught me how to shoot if I ever needed to."

"Well, then…"

"But I'm not sure I want to have a gun around my house." She thought about this for a minute, looking at the handgun I'd left on the counter when I came in. "Then again, I guess you two come as a set." This made her think.

"I appreciate that you take having a gun in the house seriously. And I didn't mean to start all this tonight. I've just been worrying with this case and all." I was at risk of going off on a complete ramble if I didn't shut my mouth, so I made myself stop talking.

Cara stared off into space for a few moments. "I'll make you a deal. Since your gun is going to be in my house, or I'm going to be in your house with your gun, then I should probably know how to use it safely. But I don't think I want to have a gun of my own right now." She said all this very solemnly. Her compromise seemed fair enough.

"Deal," I said. Being a guy, I wanted to immediately start talking about when she could get with Pete for a training session, but I wasn't a complete idiot, so I quit while I was ahead. *And what was that about moving in?* I wondered again.

We enjoyed a brief make-out session, but just before it could get interesting, Alvin finished his bone and jumped up on the couch to break things up. Cara and I both sighed and I made the mistake of looking at my watch. It turned out to be just as well.

"I've got to meet Pete. Can I have some of those cookies to go?"

"Yep," she said. "There are some in a container on the counter by the sink. If you're going to be with Pete, you better take extra."

"He'll appreciate that."

CHAPTER TWENTY-THREE

I pulled up next to Pete's car. The sun had been down for an hour by this time and the temperature was falling fast. Pete dropped into the passenger seat.

"You don't look so good," I told him.

"Yeah, thanks." He sounded stuffy. "I think I'm coming down with what the girls have had." He leaned back against the headrest, looking uncomfortable.

"Here, have a cookie," I offered. Being Pete, he couldn't resist taking a couple, but instead of inhaling them with his normal gusto he only nibbled the edge of one. Clearly the big guy wasn't feeling well.

"I can cover this if you want to go home."

"No, Tolland was right. There should be two of us. But we might just do one tonight." He was *definitely* not feeling well.

"Okay. I thought we'd go by Tony Stevenson's. He's the guy with the Stepford Wife."

"Fine," Pete muttered. I was afraid I was going to have to carry him through the interview.

Before we knocked on Stevenson's door, I used my flashlight to examine his van in the driveway.

"I can't tell for sure, but I don't think so. Pretty sure the one we saw was no minivan," Pete said.

I peered in the windows, trying to see around the glare of my light. "I don't see anything. Let's knock on the door," I said, walking away from the van. Pete shuffled along behind me, moaning occasionally. "You aren't very good at being sick," I told him.

"I'm either well or I'm dying. There isn't any in between. Right now I'm dying," he groaned.

"You can wait in the car."

"No, no. I'd rather infect everyone." His attempt at levity sounded more like a threat.

I knocked on the door. Tony's wife answered, looking a little rough around the edges, like a Stepford Wife with hard drive issues.

Once we were inside, I thought I could make out some discoloration around her neck and she seemed to be wearing more makeup below the chin than she had last time.

When Tony came into the living room, he was already agitated.

"Great, just great. She told you last night that everything was fine. Right, Tracy?"

We all turned to Mrs. Stevenson, whose cold, hard eyes seemed to be trying to come to some sort of resolution. I didn't have a clue what was going on, but I figured it was best to play along. I caught a sideways glance from Pete. He looked very confused.

"What would you like to do?" I asked her, trying to sound like I knew something I didn't.

"Oh, the hell with it, I'm out of here," she said, and in an instant Tony launched himself at her.

I moved between them just in time to be knocked to the ground. Tony came with me, but his focus was on his wife to the point that he treated me like a piece of furniture that had gotten in his way, trying to propel himself up and over me and within reach of her. I tried to grab onto him, but caught only the edge of his shirt.

Tony was back up and moving toward Tracy when I saw

Pete come thundering at him. Tony never saw Pete coming and Pete just crashed into him, taking Tony to the ground. Tony was completely out of control now and swung a fist at Pete, while Pete grabbled for him and tried to get the upper hand. Tony, we learned later, had some boxing experience, and when he landed a blow it had some power behind it. As I got to my knees, Tony managed to land a stiff uppercut to Pete's jaw. The blow would have felled a weaker man, but Pete was tough.

Just as I was finally making some progress toward the pair, Pete threw up on Tony. And not just a little bit. A lot.

"Ahhhhhhh!" Tony screamed like a girl.

I instinctively stumbled backward. Pete looked awful and was still dry-heaving as he pulled his handcuffs from their holster at his side and managed to get them on Tony. Tony, for his part, was squealing and trying to get away. Pete cuffed Tony's hands in front, which is strictly a no-no, but I figured we could take care of that before we put Tony in the car. I didn't really think I should criticize Pete on his arrest technique at this point.

"I think I'm coming down with the flu," Pete said, somewhat anticlimactically to the room. Tracy was laughing so hard I thought she might hurt herself. Tony, on the other hand, was cursing and sputtering on the floor.

"Get up," I told Tony.

"What the hell? I'm going to sue you bastards. I've got to get this crap off me!" he screamed at me.

"Don't worry. I'm going to clean you off before I put you in my car," I told him. I ran through his Miranda rights while Tracy showed Pete to a bathroom where he could clean up.

Half an hour later we'd managed to wipe Tony off enough to put him in my car. He still hadn't stopped cursing. It turned out that he and Tracy had spent the previous evening fighting so violently that the police were called twice. Tony and Tracy had mistakenly thought that we were doing a follow-up on the domestic dispute calls, assuming we were City of Calhoun police officers.

"The good news, Tony, is that this clears you in the Swamp Hacker murders." He sputtered more foul language. I looked over at Pete, who was lying against the door. "I'm taking you home," I told him.

"The girls had it last week," Pete's wife, Sarah, confirmed when I walked him to the door. "I told him he didn't look good." Sarah was one of the nicest people I'd ever met. I've never heard her say a bad thing about anyone, and she treated Pete like the world's biggest teddy bear.

"Come on, you big lunk," she told him. Pete just groaned. "Would you like to come in? I can fix you a sandwich," she said, trying to lure me inside so she could be nice to me.

"No, thanks. I have cookies in the car. And I've got the guy we arrested. I probably shouldn't leave him in there too long."

"It's not hot. He'll be fine," she said, completely straight-faced. Sarah had a very dry sense of humor.

It was a bit of a struggle to get away, but eventually Sarah let me leave after I promised to come by for dinner sometime soon.

I dropped Tony off at the jail and headed home. I spent the rest of the evening alternately writing up the report on Tony's arrest, scratching an insistent Ivy and eating cookies. Not surprisingly, I had sugar-induced nightmares where Pete taught a class at the academy that involved fighting off attackers by throwing up on them.

The next morning, I headed for the office to look over Pete's notes and come up with a game plan for the day. I wanted to re-interview Tom West and then tackle some of the names on Pete's list.

My phone started playing "Cheeseburger in Paradise" when I was halfway to the office. "Pete, how are you feeling?" I asked.

"Did I really throw up on a suspect?" he moaned.

"Yes, you did. It was a beautiful role reversal. You stood up for law enforcement officers across our great nation when you barfed on him. You have become legend."

"Yeah, thanks," he said, laughing in spite of how bad he still felt. "Are you going to interview more Hacker suspects today?"

"I'm planning on it."

"By yourself?"

"I thought I might ask Julio to go with me."

"Why don't you call Tolland?" Pete suggested.

I thought about it for a moment. "Not a bad idea. I'll give him a call."

"I've got a file of written notes on my desk, and I just emailed you my interview reports. I'll try and make it in tomorrow."

"Don't worry, we'll cover for you. Just rest."

When I hung up with Pete, I called Tolland and he seemed eager to come over. He had two other investigators working on the leads in Leon County. He said he'd meet me at our office in an hour, giving me plenty of time to go over Pete's files.

Tolland looked uncomfortable in the passenger seat. It had taken him a minute to accept that it made sense for me to drive since I knew the area better. To help him relax, I decided to pick his brain about the previous murders.

"Did you and Dad actually work together much on the original cases, or was it all just a matter of sharing information?"

"Mostly sharing information, just 'cause we both were busy. But I knew your dad before we were on the case together."

"Really?"

"We went through the law enforcement academy together, and I worked my first two years as a policeman in

Calhoun. Of course, your dad got on with the sheriff's office, so we saw each other a bit during that time."

I looked over at Tolland and tried to imagine him and my dad as rookies. It was hard to picture them as cadets fresh from the academy. I could only imagine how much they both had changed. It wasn't just the nature of the work that beat you down, but also the constant politics of the job. Law enforcement officers are battered on all sides, which is why we tend to defend each other so fiercely. Who else is there to count on?

"I guess you could tell me some wild stories about Dad?" I prompted, hoping to get some good blackmail material to use against the old man the next time he got all high and mighty with me.

"Your dad? Ha! Honestly, most of the guys didn't like him. Well, that's a little rough. He was just a little too… righteous for most of the other guys. Which got him in trouble sometimes. He'd do what was right instead of following the letter of the law, or what was accepted as standard procedure by everyone else."

"Both literally and figuratively, he sits on a high horse sometimes," I grumbled.

"That sense of right and wrong is important in an officer. You know, you have a lot of discretionary power when you're on the street. Knowing when to enforce the law and when to bend it is important. I had to learn it. Your dad had the concept down from day one. A couple of months after we both started, we rolled up separately to a fight at the Fast Mart. It pretty much broke up as soon as they saw us drive into the parking lot. We got the two guys who were fighting into my car, no problem. One of the bystanders was also a regular offender, always looking for anything he could smoke or snort. Gutter was his street name. Anyway, he didn't have the sense that God gave a rock, and because he didn't like the two guys who were fighting, he'd decided to hang around and make fun of them being arrested.

"Long story short, he was laughing and calling them

names and at the same time pulling up his pants. Well, a small gem bag of drugs fell onto the ground right in front of your dad and me. Gutter looked at us like he'd just messed his pants, which he had, so to speak. I was waiting for your dad to grab him. Drug collars were looked on very favorably. But instead, Ted looked Gutter square in the eye, reached down, picked up the little bag and said, 'You need to learn about a thing called Karma. Laughing at other peoples' misfortunes isn't a nice thing to do. Now get out of here.'"

"Keep that to yourself. That story wouldn't help Dad get reelected," I said.

"Yeah, I was pretty disgusted at the time too. But not a month later, I learned it was Gutter who warned Ted about a little ambush some guys had set up for your father. So I don't know if Gutter studied up on Karma or not, but after that Gutter became one of your dad's go-to informants. Not that Gutter still didn't get arrested from time to time, and not that your father wouldn't do the arresting if he needed to, but there wasn't a need to on that day at that time. That's what took me years to learn. You have to learn when you need to arrest someone and when you don't."

We were getting close to our destination. "That's the Southside Car Recycling Center. Also known as the Junkyard," I said, pointing ahead. We were hoping to catch Tom West at work. "His alibi for the last killing was a prostitute by the name of Trixie. She verified that he visited her, but her drug habit is so bad that I doubt she can tell night from day, let alone what day of the week it was."

It turned out that Tom was the manager. He came out of the back and pulled us outside.

"So now you come to my work! Can't you bastards ever leave a guy alone?"

"Where were you Tuesday night?"

"I haven't killed anyone. I'm not a murderer," he growled, which was not an answer to my question.

"Just tell us where you were. And don't say Trixie. I checked her out. You have great taste in women, but she's lucky if she remembers what year it is," I told him.

"I'm screwed. I was playing a game last night, online, but I'm guessing you all ain't gonna take my login and game time information as proof of anything," he said sullenly.

"You got that right," Tolland said. He was standing back, letting me do most of the questioning, but, like my dad, his presence was hard to ignore. I noticed that West's eyes kept drifting to the most authoritative figure among us, and that wasn't me. I shifted closer and got between them, forcing West to focus on me.

"Do you have access to a van?" I put my hand up before he could answer. "This is very important. If you lie to us about this, we're going to take that as evidence of your guilt." He was rolling his eyes and shifting from foot to foot.

"And if I say I do? I know how this goes. You're setting a damn trap. I go left, you go left. I go right, you go right. Whatever I do, I lose." West was getting himself worked up, his breathing shallow. I swear I could see his heart pounding in his chest.

"Just calm down. We want to catch a killer. We aren't here to screw with you. Take a minute. You got family?" I asked him.

This question caught him off guard, causing him to look at me and wonder if he'd heard right. "Family?"

"Do you have parents who are alive? Wife? Ex-wife?"

"I have my mom. Dad's dead. Two ex-wives."

"Hell, you're a novice. I got four exes," Tolland joked.

"Any kids?" I asked West.

"One. He's all grown up. Let me guess, you want to see the van too." He had calmed down a bit and was apparently not interested in engaging in small talk, which suited me.

"Where is it?"

"Out back. We use it for small deliveries." He turned and headed around the side of the building.

The three of us trooped out back to a small gravel parking area. The van was white, older and pretty battered up. I walked around, trying to see it from different angles.

We all curse eyewitnesses, and wonder why they can't be more observant, but as soon as you're walking in their shoes the anger turns to frustration with your own powers of observation and the fallibility of memory. It's possible that this was the van we saw, but it seemed equally possible it wasn't.

I took out my phone and took several pictures so that we could show them to any witnesses.

"Can we look inside?" I asked.

There was a pregnant pause that stretched out for a while, but then he nodded. "Go ahead."

I opened up the double doors in back while Tolland went to the driver's side door. The rear of the van was a large open space with metal shelves along both sides. I couldn't have touched anything inside without getting my hand stained with grease. There were old motor parts, pieces of wire and tools lying all over the bed and stacked on the shelves. Along with all the other junk, there were fast food bags, plastic Coke bottles and beer cans scattered around.

I almost deleted the photos then and there. This couldn't have been the van that the body was in. If someone had put a body in this van, it would have had grease and who knew what other stuff on it. Also, I don't think it would be possible to take a body out of this van without leaving a small pile of junk behind.

"Do you have access to any other van?" I asked West. He seemed surprised that I wasn't more interested in this one.

"No. Nope." He shook his head.

"You don't go to a church with a van you could use, or have a neighbor, friend or relative that has a van?"

"Damn it. I'm sure I know someone who has a van. Who doesn't?" He was getting worked up again.

"Okay, fair point. Have you ever borrowed anyone else's van?"

He actually paused to think about it. "No. Maybe years ago to move or something."

"But not in the last couple of years? And remember what

192

I said about lying."

"I swear I haven't borrowed any van in years." He shook his head emphatically. Reluctantly, I believed him.

CHAPTER TWENTY-FOUR

We left the Junkyard and headed to the first of Pete's suspects.

"This next one is a guy who's been in and out of jail. He's on the sexual predator list, but he's off of parole right now. Being out of jail and off parole is unusual for him. I figured it up, and he's spent eighty percent of his adult life under correctional supervision."

"Charmer."

"Yep, Craig Leigh is the kind of guy who gives criminals a bad name."

"I'm assuming he was out of jail when both sets of murders took place?" Tolland asked rhetorically.

"I think the only reason I don't like him for these is that they aren't cruel enough, and there doesn't seem to be a sexual component. Both of which are hallmarks of his MO. He was caught committing a robbery ten years ago because he couldn't resist fondling a customer in the store he was robbing."

"Dirt bag," Tolland spit out.

"Exactly. Not surprisingly, he can't find a job so we should be able to find him at the halfway house he's living in."

"Aren't they for people on parole?"

"He couldn't find anywhere else to stay, so they're letting him do work around the place for board. Honestly, if we can't get him to move out of the county, it's the second best option. He's required to sign in and out, there are random drug tests and his room is subject to unannounced searches. Pete said the supervisor reported that Craig has followed all the rules, but does stay out pretty late sometimes. Since he doesn't have a curfew, that's not seen as a problem."

"Does he have a car?"

"Not under his name. But he has access to a number of cars owned by family. He has two brothers and a sister and, according to the interview that Pete did with him, he's borrowed cars and trucks from all of them."

"You'd think they'd cut the scumbag off."

"You would, but the rest of the family aren't model citizens themselves. One of the brothers and the sister have had drug problems, and the other brother works as a rental property manager for the Thompsons."

"'Nough said."

"Four ex-wives? Or were you just saying that to make West feel better?" I asked Tolland, giving him a bit of whiplash with the subject change.

"I've the scars to prove it. Literal scars in the case of two of them."

"That must have made your life interesting."

"Interesting like the Chinese curse. What can I say? I wasn't lucky like your dad."

"You knew Mom?"

"I did. I even saw you once or twice when you were small enough to still be carried around."

"That was a few years ago."

"Honestly, I say lucky, but your dad was smart. He met your mom and he never looked for anyone else."

"I appreciate hearing that." *Especially after the way he was making eyes at my old babysitter*, I thought.

"Being a cop or a deputy puts temptation in your face all

the time. Not many take money or drugs, stuff like that, but more than a few take a little fun when it's offered."

"You ever take advantage?" I asked, not sure I wanted to hear the answer.

"Never when I was on duty. Though I won't deny that I met a few women on duty who were willing to meet me off duty for a little fun. Trust me, I earned my four ex-wives."

We pulled into a parking lot that served four duplexes. I'd called ahead and a man in a Jeep Cherokee stepped out when we pulled up.

"Manuel Marco," he said, walking up to Tolland, who shook his hand.

"I'm Cedrick Tolland with the Leon County Sheriff's Office. I'm just sitting in on the interview. Deputy Macklin is the lead on this case," Tolland said, turning to me.

"Sorry," Marco said. We shook hands, and he turned toward the duplexes. "If you'll follow me. We have eight apartments with two to four residents in each. We're lucky we have this. It's not easy to find a place that is far enough away from schools and playgrounds that we can house someone on the sex offender list," he said.

I cringed. I knew that released sex offenders had met their legal obligations and that some of them were convicted of offenses that should not have landed them on the list in the first place—like a teenager who took a picture of himself naked and was convicted of being in possession of child pornography. But some of those people were terrifying and were out of prison only because they were able to avoid the worse charges. Sometimes the laws protect the guilty.

"How long has he been here?"

"Craig has been helping out here since he finished his probation two years ago. He lives in unit one," Marco said.

"Have you ever seen him drive a light-colored van?" I asked as we came up to the door of his duplex.

"I can't remember. I know he's always borrowing vehicles. His switching vehicles caused some trouble at first. We keep an eye on who comes and goes, and we were getting reports of different vehicles. Once we figured out that it was Craig borrowing cars from his family, it was cool We gave him a marked parking space so we'd know, okay, that's Craig's car of the week or whatever." He knocked on the door. No answer. He knocked again and a big guy with a crew cut whose face was covered by tattoos finally opened the door.

"Oh, hey, Mr. Marco," the man said in a polite tone that seemed at odds with the prison tattoos.

"What's up, Mickey? Is Craig here?"

Mickey poked his head out and looked around. "He's out working. Hey, I got a problem with…" Mickey went on to tell Marco about some issue he had with his employer. We heard a leaf blower start up around back of the duplexes.

"That's him," Marco told us.

"We'll find him," I said.

"Good deal. If you need anything, just call me." Marco turned back to Mickey and went into the duplex with him.

We circled around back and found Craig blowing leaves off of the heat pumps behind the duplex.

"Yeah, what do you guys want?" he said after he'd turned off the blower and taken off his earmuffs.

"Just want to ask you a few questions."

"Always," he snarled, but he set the blower down. "What?"

"Where were you Tuesday night?"

"Tuesday… I was here."

"All night?"

"Yeah, off and on."

"What does off and on mean?"

"I went out for smokes. Maybe a beer. Mostly, I was here." He looked at me with the dead eyes of a hardened criminal. He was a professional-level liar, so the only way to know if he was telling the truth was to get corroboration.

"Who else saw you?"

"Mickey. He lives in the same apartment. We watched a basketball game for a while. Yeah, I got him some smokes too."

"Where'd you buy the cigarettes and beer?"

"The Fast Mart by the railroad tracks."

"You drive or walk?"

"Drove."

"What car did you drive?"

"Same one that's out there now. That piece of crap Taurus."

"Have you had access to or driven a van in the last month?"

"Nope. Just that Taurus."

I thought about asking where he got the Taurus, but it really didn't matter. We let him get back to work, and we went to talk with Mickey and Marco again. Nothing they said contradicted Craig.

I put checking the Fast Lane's CCTV on my to-do list. I called them and told the manager I'd want to look at Tuesday night's footage. Management at the Fast Mart was pretty cooperative since their store probably accounted for ten percent of our calls.

"Lunch?" I asked Tolland when we got back to the car.

"Sounds good."

"Why haven't we found Jillian's car?" Tolland asked me while we were waiting on our food at Deep Pit Bar-b-que. "Almost all of the abductions took place near the victim's car. You've had your people and the Calhoun police looking for a couple of days. So where's the car?"

I thought about this for a few moments. "It's not in Leon?"

"Nothing's shown up on our BOLO yet. We probably need to expand it to counties within a hundred miles. Other possibilities?"

"The car is somewhere where it's not easy to see. Maybe she parked it in a private garage or put a cover over it. Though neither seems likely."

"Private garage. Like she went to visit a friend and parked in their garage?"

"Unlikely. She didn't have many friends. At least not close friends, and by everyone's account she didn't have a boyfriend or girlfriend. And, besides, unless they're the killer they would have noticed that her car was still in their garage. Maybe a private parking garage?" I suggested, and then responded to my own suggestion. "Not that we have any in Adams County."

Tolland pulled out a notebook and made a note. "I'll ask the Tallahassee police to have their patrols check out all the parking garages in town."

"Of course…" I saw where Tolland had been leading me. "Maybe the killer hid the car or disposed of it somewhere."

"Why?"

"Because, unlike the other murders, there was something about the car that might have given him away."

"I think that's very likely. He's getting sloppier."

"Something about the car. Maybe he got in it and was afraid that we'd find DNA or fingerprints."

"Maybe. But I think there's a real possibility that he couldn't leave it to be found where it was."

Our food arrived, so we quit talking and gave our barbecue the attention it deserved.

"So I hear you don't want to be a deputy anymore?" Tolland asked when we were both finished with the majority of our lunch.

"I'm not that good at it," I said, a bit irritated that someone—most likely Dad—had been talking about me.

"That's not what I've heard," he stated.

"I almost got people killed last month."

"Hell, I almost got someone killed when I ran through a yellow light last week. The world is a dangerous place."

"That's not the same thing."

"Look, the truth is you take the job seriously. You aren't some yahoo running around enjoying the privileges that a gun and badge can give you. You understand that it's about respect for the law, duty and responsibility for the men and women you work with, as well as for the people you are sworn to protect. That's a good thing. Of course, you're smart so you over-think everything. You have to learn to compartmentalize better, that's all."

"I'm not like a lot of the other deputies," I said, shaking my head and trying to figure a way out of this line of questioning.

"Neither was your father. That's what I was trying to get at earlier. Sure, he always wanted to be in law enforcement, but he came at it from a different angle than most of us. Your dad has always been about the community. He's a great sheriff because he sees the whole picture, not just the law enforcement side of it."

"I don't want to end up living a life of regrets. I see the burden that the job has been to Dad."

"We all have regrets. Like this case. I know your dad regrets not catching this bastard, but I'll bet every penny my ex-wives took from me that he has never regretted hunting the SOB." Tolland let that hang in the air for a moment. "Okay, I've busted your balls enough. What's on tap for this afternoon?"

"We've got a couple more on Pete's suspect list."

"I'm game. There are four investigators with our office checking Leon County suspects for their whereabouts on Tuesday. If none of us comes up with a smoking gun, my suggestion is that we bring everyone together for a meeting to brainstorm the case."

"More ideas couldn't hurt."

"Exactly."

We paid and left. We may not have had much of a plan, but at least it was a plan.

Both of the afternoon's interviews all but cleared the individuals, so Tolland and I agreed to put a meeting together. He said he'd like to bring his people over to Adams County so that he could show them the locations of the abductions and where the victims lived. We also agreed that a meeting afterhours and away from our offices would provide the most distraction-free environment for everyone.

After Tolland left, I called Pete. He assured me that he was feeling better and would be back on his feet in a couple of days. I filled him in on all the interviews. He suggested that we have the meeting in Winston's back room so it was on neutral ground and casual enough to help everyone open up.

CHAPTER TWENTY-FIVE

By Sunday afternoon, not much had changed except that Pete was officially declared a flu survivor and everything was a go for our Monday evening meeting. Jillian Grey's car was still missing. We had compiled a list of the farms, stores and restaurants that Homegrown worked with and conducted interviews at most of them, but we still hadn't come up with any leads.

Cara and I were taking a walk around my property, enjoying the sun and the cool winter afternoon. We held hands as we walked and watched Alvin sniff every tree and bush.

"It must be awful to be hunting someone as dangerous as this… maniac and not have anything to go on," Cara said, squeezing my hand. I knew she'd brought it up because I wasn't having much luck keeping my mind on anything else. I kept wondering what we might have missed.

"I'm sorry. I know I haven't been very good company today," I apologized.

"I'm not complaining. I understand, really."

"We're doing everything we can, but the leads have dried up. There's a lot of forensic evidence that's been collected, but most of it isn't going to do us any good until we arrest someone."

"Can't you eliminate some of your suspects since you already have their DNA? You do, right?" she asked.

It felt very strange talking to Cara about the case. And I had to be careful not to tell her anything that we were holding back from the public. Not that I didn't trust her, but if something did leak and there was an investigation, I'd want to be able to say I hadn't told anyone.

"You're right. We have DNA from the more hardcore suspects who've been arrested in the last ten years or so. The problem is that we don't have a DNA sample that we know conclusively is from the killer."

"That makes sense."

"We've got our meeting tomorrow evening. I'm hoping we'll come out of it with at least a few good ideas on how to move forward. But there aren't any guarantees. Maybe we'll all get in the room and argue for three hours. Many murderers have walked free because of the incompetence of the investigators."

She bumped into to me playfully. "I have confidence in you."

"We've got a lot of great investigators in the area."

"Is it okay if I think of you as one of them?"

"It's a foolish choice on your part, but I guess it's okay," I told her with a smile.

"You really kind of like this work, don't you?"

"Some days. I like it better when I catch the bad guy."

"So, really, you just quit because you got scared." Coming out of the blue like that, what she said should have made me mad, but it didn't. She said it so softly and with such compassion that I had to admit she was mostly right.

"Yeah, kind of. Scared that I was going to get someone killed," I said.

"Your dad's a pretty good sheriff, isn't he?" she asked.

"I hate to admit it sometimes, but he's one of the best I've seen."

"He doesn't cut you any special slack because you're his

son, does he?"

I stopped and pulled her around. "Okay, what are you driving at?" I said quizzically.

"Answer the question. Does your father treat you any differently than anyone else?" Cara demanded, smiling at me.

"You know, you could quit your job at the vet and go to law school," I said and she hit me lightly in the chest. "Okay, okay. He does treat me differently. Dad's tougher on me because I'm his son."

"So don't you think he'd fire you if he thought you were a danger to anyone? Or incompetent?"

I took both her shoulders in my hands and looked her squarely in the eyes. "Where are you going with this?" I asked gently, knowing exactly what she was getting at, but not wanting to admit it.

"It seems clear to everyone else that you aren't some loose cannon about to bash through the side of the ship and destroy everything. So you're just using that as an excuse. If you don't want to be a deputy anymore, that's fine, but I want you to be sure that's what you want. You need to be really honest with yourself."

I pulled her into a hug. "I don't know for sure what I want," I said as she squeezed me tightly. "Let me catch this monster first and then we'll see."

On Monday Pete and I followed up on a few leads that had come in over the weekend—mostly people who thought they had seen Jillian or her car on Tuesday night. During the afternoon we worked on a presentation for the meeting at Winston's. Pete had already arranged to use the back room for the meeting and Winston had even offered to serve pastries and coffee for everyone.

At six o'clock Pete and I packed everything up and headed over to the restaurant to get set up for the meeting. By seven we had a room full of investigators and forensic technicians, including Marcus. Dad had reluctantly excluded

Shantel since she had a personal stake in the crimes, which a defense attorney could use against us if we ever got to a trial.

Cedrick Tolland came up to me. "Your dad on his way?"

"He had to drop Mauser off with Jamie, the dog sitter. His car's in the shop."

"That dog." Tolland shook his head. "I remember you all having those monsters years ago."

"Mom swore she felt better when one of our Great Danes was watching me than when she left me with Dad. Of course, they were all better trained than Mauser."

Dad finally came charging through the door.

"Sorry, folks. Grab some coffee real quick and find a seat. Rick, why don't you come up here with us."

Tolland came to the front of the room and stood with Dad, Pete and me. Once everyone had found a seat, Dad looked at the dry-erase boards we'd set up. One of them listed all the original murders. Dad went over to it.

"Tolland and I are not here as your supervisors. Our primary reason for being here is because we were the lead investigators on the original set of murders. And this meeting is taking place because we failed. We couldn't find the man who committed those atrocities. But I look around this room and I'm reassured. I see men and women who are dedicated, professional and probably a lot smarter than me, and maybe even smarter than Tolland." There were a few chuckles. "Now I'm going to turn this over to the current lead investigators Tolland, Macklin and Henley."

There was an agreement to focus on the new murders and we went over each of them thoroughly. We had representatives from all specialties—investigative, crime scene and lab tech—and each was able to give their take on the individual murders. Many of the folks in the room had only been privy to the facts that had to do with their specialties, but by talking about all the evidence together we were able to get some different perspectives.

The van was now front and center in the investigation because it was a solid piece of evidence that we could look for. Tolland had invited some of the Leon County tech guys and they had come up with some algorithms to narrow down the search through VIN records, the DMV and automotive service providers to provide us with some quality lists of vans in the area. While I didn't fully understand how it all worked, I had hopes that it might lead to something.

Next we created a chart of the women's movements and locations. Each of them had some connection to a restaurant or bar. How did that figure in? Since they didn't all work at the same place or visit the same place, vans connected to various service industries would be a priority.

One of our IT guys reported on the results of his search of the online files for recurring names. So far, nothing stood out. We all felt like we were looking for someone who would be trying to stay close to the investigation, though it could always be a person who was associated with it by virtue of their job. I think all of us cringed when we were forced to admit that it could have been someone in law enforcement. It was always a possibility.

By ten-thirty we were all about brain-dead. We'd agreed on some actionable tasks, which we assigned to the most capable people. We also agreed to meet again in two weeks if we hadn't uncovered any evidence that broke the case open.

The meeting ended and we said our goodbyes. As Pete and I gathered up our materials, Winston and Mary came in and started cleaning up the dishes.

"Appreciate everything," Pete said to them.

"No problem. You all figure anything out?" Winston asked as he emptied plates and passed them to Mary.

"You know, it's all footwork and phone calls. Or, these days, it's all emails and texts. Just going to take time. You all have been a big help."

"Anything for my best customer! Come in tomorrow evening, bring the wife and girls, and I'll cook you the best prime rib in town." Winston smiled and handed Mary a glass. "Mary will bake you her special chocolate chip pecan pie."

"Sure," Mary said with a little less enthusiasm than her father. She looked tired.

"Jamie's coming with the van," Dad said as he walked by, his phone in hand. "Walk out with me."

I turned and fell in step with him. "You didn't drive?"

"I had Jamie drop me off so he could take Mauser for a doggie sundae at Buster's."

"Spoiled dog," I muttered.

Dad ignored me. "I feel good about our progress. During the first investigation there was tension between the two departments. Things are different this time around."

"That's good. A lot of that is because of you," I told him, and it was true. I'd never seen Dad compromise an investigation because he felt territorial. He was the first to reach out and share information and research. "I can't help but feel like we're not seeing something. Something right in front of our faces." Something was lurking in the dark recesses of my brain, but I couldn't get a focus on it.

"I've felt like that with most of the major investigations I've worked on. Sometimes it turns out to be true, but other times there just wasn't anything there to be seen. The feeling is the same when you're working on any difficult problem. You always think that the solution is just out of reach. Maybe that's the way our minds motivate us to keep working when we have a seemingly impossible task."

"Actually, that makes some sense," I agreed.

Jamie pulled up in Dad's van. He got out and, after attaching the leash to Mauser's harness, brought him out of the van. Mauser dragged Jamie over to Dad and me. The big goof could just barely be contained from jumping on us. I'm embarrassed to admit that I indulged him in some ear rubs, baby talk and side pats.

"I guess you deserve a little special attention after that death ride in the van the other night," I told the dog, who leaned into me as he ate up the sympathy.

Jamie took him for a walk while I went back and helped Pete carry out the boxes and supplies that we'd brought.

After we got the car loaded, Dad came over to say goodbye. As a parting gift, he handed me a doggie pickup bag.

"Would you mind throwing this away?" he said and turned away before I could say no.

"Damn," I grumbled.

"What?" Pete asked. "Oh. Never mind. I'll wait here," he said and got in the car.

"I'm going around back to throw this in a dumpster," I told Pete. I don't know if he heard me. His face was illuminated by his phone as he texted away with someone.

I walked around the to the back of the restaurant, giving a quick wave to Mary as she walked out to her car. The streetlights shown brightly on the back of the building. There wasn't a lot of noise. Calhoun shuts down after about ten on weeknights, especially on a cold winter's night.

Behind the building was an unloading area for the produce, meat and kitchen supplies they ordered. A panel van was parked near the back door, with prominent signs reading *Winston's Grill, Only the best!* on either side. The restaurant door opened and Winston came out, carrying a couple bags of garbage.

"Hey!" I said and he turned and looked my way. I'd surprised him, but he managed to give me a smile.

I held up the bag with Mauser's deposit in it. "I need to drop this in your dumpster. Dad walked Mauser before he went home."

Winston, like just about everyone in town, was familiar with Mauser, so he chuckled. "No problem. I appreciate your dad picking it up. Dumpster's over here," he said, pointing.

I went around the back of the van while Winston crossed between the van and the building. We met at the dumpster and I held it open so he could throw the two garbage bags in and then I tossed Mauser's bag after them.

"See ya. Thanks again," I told Winston.

"Hey, take care," he said, heading back toward the gap between the front of the van and the wall. He wasn't walking very fast and I could sympathize. It must have been hard on the joints of a man his age—late fifties?—standing at a stove all day.

I started to go around the back of the van when something caught my eye. There was something off on one corner of the sign on that side of the van. I detoured over to have a look. *Odd*, I thought. When I was about a foot from it I realized that the sign was actually magnetic and could be put on and taken off at will. I reached out to touch the corner that was sticking up a little and then the van started moving rapidly toward my face.

Then it became clear that it was me that was moving, not the van, as my head slammed into the side of the vehicle, hard. Winston grabbed my back and slammed me against the van again, my side taking the impact this time. I fell to the ground, reaching for my Glock 17 handgun, but I landed on that same side and needed to roll over before I could draw the gun.

As I rolled, Winston dropped his full weight down on top of me, focused on preventing me from getting the gun. He had one knee on my left arm and the other on my thigh, but I still managed to get my hand to my holster. In desperation, Winston bent forward and bit into my arm, seemingly intent on taking out a chunk of my flesh.

Only the fact that I was wearing a jacket saved me from losing half a pound of meat. The pain was excruciating and, despite my determination, my right hand let go of the grip enough that he was able to pull my hand away from the gun. The Glock fell out of my holster onto the ground beside me. I saw Winston look at it and start to go for it. The only recourse I had was to roll on top of the handgun. As soon as I did that, he began punching me mercilessly in the ribs and head.

I know that I was screaming for help, but I honestly didn't hear myself. Later I'd realize that I'd been counting on a man sitting in a car and texting to save me. If I had thought about it at that moment, I probably would have just given up.

Some small functioning part of my brain suggested that it would be a good idea to try to crawl under the van. Slowly, between punches, I inched my way under the vehicle. If Winston had stopped to think for a moment, he could have just slammed my head into the pavement or stomped on it and it would have been all over. Luckily for me, rational sense had already left the battlefield.

At last I managed to maneuver most of the way under the van, but the gun hadn't moved with me, leaving it exposed between us. Winston and I both grabbed for the gun at the same time. I was able to get my hands on it first, but before I could get it pointed in a useful direction, Winston tried to use his strong hands and arms to drag me back out from under the van.

Then I saw an image that has come back to haunt me in my nightmares. Unable to pull me out or to pry the gun out of my grasp, Winston laid down on the pavement, pulled at my hands and tried to get his face down close enough to bite me. Bathed in the streetlights, his gnashing teeth were a mere inch from my hands. The scene was surreal, as if I'd fallen straight into a zombie movie.

I tried to resist, but he kept pulling, my bare hands getting a little closer to his teeth with every second. I felt myself weakening and I swear that I could feel his hot breath on my hand. Then my ears rang with a noise that sounded like an air horn had been blasted under the van.

I found out later that Pete had started to wonder where I was and came looking for me. Being a pretty quick thinker, he sized up the situation and landed a full-footed kick to Winston's crotch. It was Winston's scream that had almost busted my eardrums. Pete pulled him away from the van, cuffing him easily as Winston was already on his stomach and no longer in a fighting frame of mind.

I just lay under the van, trying to recover, until Pete came over and peered down at me. "You okay?" he asked, sounding worried.

"Not sure yet. Just give me a minute," I told him. Pete kept looking at me. "Okay." I put out my arms and Pete took them, pulling me out as I stifled a grunt of pain.

I sat on the ground, holding my sides and looking at Winston, who was breathing hard and occasionally moaning. I wanted nothing more than to go over to him and give him some swift kicks in the ribs, but I just sat there. It hurt to breathe.

"What the hell?" Pete asked. I pointed up at the sign on the van. Pete stared at it, then all of a sudden he turned, moved away from me and threw up.

"Are you okay?" I asked him, puzzled. I thought he was over the flu.

"No! No, I'm *not* okay." Pete dry-heaved onto the pavement some more. "I've eaten food that was delivered in that van. That… that…" He was pointing back at Winston. "That monster fed me meals."

"I see your point. Damn, I hope he didn't use the same cleaver," I said, letting my morbid sense of humor get the best of me. That thought sent Pete into a whole other round of dry-heaves.

Recovered somewhat, Pete came back over to me. I struggled to get to my feet and managed it with his help.

"I'll call for cars and our crime scene techs… and an ambulance," Pete said, looking at me.

"No, not yet," I told him and he gave me a funny look.

"Surely we can't kill him?" he asked with an expression that harbored hope.

"No, we aren't going to kill him. But we aren't going to arrest him either." Now I really had Pete's attention. I pulled out my phone. "I'm calling Dad. You call Tolland." Pete's face broke into a broad smile.

CHAPTER TWENTY-SIX

Forty-five minutes later Tolland and Dad were standing over Winston, who had recovered enough that he was sputtering about his rights and police abuse.

"I'll be damned," Tolland said for the third time.

"I got lucky," I said.

"Hell, I'd rather have luck than skill any day of the week," Tolland said, patting me on the back. I tried hard not to wince.

"Yeah, but after all of those interviews and boxes of evidence, it came down to me walking back here to throw Mauser's bag in the dumpster." I was shaking my head in wonder.

Dad reached out and gripped my upper arm. When I turned to him all he said was, "Thank you."

Dad and Tolland called in the crime scene techs from both Adams and Leon Counties, as well as the Florida Department of Law Enforcement. They were not going to cut any corners with this one.

After a short while Marcus came out of the restaurant carrying the baseball bat that Winston had kept under the front counter.

"Years ago he told me he kept a bat by the cash register in case someone tried to rob him. I never even thought about it," Dad said, shaking his head. We were all doing a lot of head shaking that night.

Pete came over to us, looking concerned. "What're you thinking?" I asked him.

"Mary. She couldn't have known, could she?" His expression made it clear that he didn't know whether to feel sorry for her or to consider her in the same dark light as her father.

"I don't know," I said honestly.

"We'll have to bring her in for questioning. The sooner, the better. If she is involved, we don't want to give her time to destroy evidence at his house," Dad said.

"I'll go pick her up," Pete said solemnly.

At that point I finally let the ambulance take me to Tallahassee for X-rays. On the way I called Cara; I was actually looking forward to telling her about this little adventure.

Shantel surprised me by showing up at the hospital. She really wanted to give me a hug, but I waved her off with a small grimace.

"Pain, and a lot of it," I told her.

"I haven't told Tonya yet, but she'll be thrilled. She hasn't been saying much, but I know that guy still being on the loose was freaking her out."

"Understandable." I was waiting to be wheeled down to X-ray. "Did you make a special trip over here?"

"I heard it all on the scanner. And then Marcus called me. I can't be at the scene, of course." She held up her hand. "I know your dad is just thinking of the case, I got no problem with that. But I wanted to tell you personally how grateful Tonya and I are. Now you're coming back to work full time. I won't hear of anything else." Shantel pinned me down with her eyes, hard as steel.

"Okay," my mouth said before my brain had a chance to stop it.

"Least that's settled. Now that I know about Winston, I got to thinking. You know Tonya went to the Grill looking for a job."

"I remember," I said.

"When you all were questioning her the other day, she remembered a familiar smell right before he clubbed her. I bet you anything she smelled that grill on him."

"You're probably right. Smell is one of our most resilient senses. It was another clue that would have helped us find him sooner if we'd understood what it meant."

"You want a Coke or something?" Shantel asked. She spent the rest of the night babysitting me and finally drove me back to my car at four in the morning. Nothing was broken, just very bruised. I was grateful that my coat had kept him from breaking the skin on my arm when he bit me. Still, there was a bruise in the shape of his mouth. The faster that went away, the happier I'd be.

I got a couple of hours' sleep before deciding that I needed to go into the office and help wrap things up. I called Cara on my way into town. She was just getting ready to take her lunch break, so I swung by the vet's office and picked her up.

"Let me guess where we *aren't* going for lunch," she said.

"Don't even joke about that. Poor Pete's going to be lost without that place."

"How are *you* doing?" She gently touched my side and I winced. "I would have come to the hospital."

"It was bad enough that I woke you up."

"I'd have been pretty pissed if you hadn't called."

"Shantel shepherded me through all the hospital hoops. I've got some pills for the pain, but I'm not going to take them unless I can't sleep." I hesitated, wondering how to tell her the next part. Finally I just blurted it out: "I've decided to go back to work at the sheriff's office full time."

She looked at me for a moment, then smiled. "Just as well. You were awful at looking for a job."

"Where do you want to go for lunch?"

"Since our choices are somewhat limited, I think I'll stick with the yogurt I have back at the vet's. I really just wanted to see you." She leaned against me, but a sharp pain caused me to gasp. "Sorry, sorry!" she said, sitting back up and taking my hand in hers instead.

After dropping her off, I headed to the sheriff's office. I was moving slowly, but the pats on the back and smiles from everyone helped. I found Pete sitting at his desk, typing up reports.

He looked up. "Finally decided to crawl into work?" he asked, smiling.

"If you'd gotten there a little earlier I'd be in much better shape. Besides, the only reason you're here so early is because Winston's is closed," I shot back.

Pete shook his head sadly. "Who would have thought that we had a killer serving us food? Hell, giving us free coffee."

"Winston liked being close to law enforcement. Close to the investigation. He probably would have given us more free meals to keep us coming in."

"Makes me sick to think about him chopping up food the same way he chopped up his victims." Pete shuddered. "I knew we were looking for a psychopath, but to find out that the psychopath was someone I considered a friend…"

"It's more convenient when the bad guy *acts* like a bad guy. And to be fair, most murderous psychopaths don't blend in as well as someone like Bundy or Winston did. They are the exception," I told him, trying to convince myself as much as Pete that serial killers weren't hiding around every corner.

"And he stopped killing for years."

"Did he give you any explanation when you processed him last night?"

"Gave it all up. We were there for four hours while he rattled on about how he'd carried out all of the killings. Funny though, he got a little touchy when we started asking about his childhood and first assaults. He admitted that he'd been picked up as a juvenile for clubbing some other kid in elementary school, and for starting a fire when he was a little older. Said he loved animals, though. Swore he'd never hurt an animal. Seemed to be point of pride."

"Our neighborhood killer was pet-friendly. Guess we should be grateful for small favors." I shook my head.

"Where Winston really got touchy was when Lt. Johnson asked him about why he targeted the people he did."

Pete paused.

"And?" I prodded him.

"I was just thinking of what it was like when I was in high school. You aren't going to believe this, but women weren't exactly fighting over me. Rejection is painful, but normal people can get over it. Being without normal empathy, Winston was furious at the women that rejected him and saw them as less than human. He harbored that anger for a long time, even after he finally found someone to love and started a family with her.

"He said the original murders happened during a rough patch in their marriage. He blamed the stress of running a business and having a young daughter. He needed an outlet for his anger, but he loved his wife too much to hurt her. So he took his frustrations out on people that reminded him of the women that had scorned him... Some had similar facial features, one of them was wearing a coat that triggered him, that sort of thing. Oddly, this helped to stabilize him and he was able to work through his issues with his wife. He really put her up on a pedestal. "

"And everything was fine until their marriage fell apart for good. She's lucky he didn't kill her."

"Winston still holds her up as a good woman. But when she left him, he felt rejected again. He projected his anger at her onto those old images of rejection and his ego demanded that he kill again to restore his confidence."

"Thank God he's locked up. Now comes the paperwork."

"We found Jillian's car. It was in a shed on Winston's property. He drove it home instead of his car Tuesday night. Turns out, Jillian had stopped by the restaurant to see if Winston would be interested in buying his produce from Homegrown. He kills her, dumps her body, gets chased by us, then realizes that he can't leave the car near the restaurant so he drives it home."

"How did he get to work the next day?"

"He told Mary that he'd had some drinks after work and a friend drove him home. She didn't think too much of it because he'd done it before. In fact, after her mom left, he got to drinking a lot, and she'd encouraged him to get rides home if he was drunk. So she drove him in on Wednesday."

"Do you think she knew anything about the murders?"

"She knew something was wrong, but he'd been weird and moody before. Depressed. Bouts of drinking. He'd actually seemed better and more stable since the killings started back up, so she says she wasn't looking a gift horse in the mouth."

"What do you think?"

He sighed. "We didn't find any evidence in plain sight at the house. Maybe she suspected. But I'm pretty sure she didn't know that he was the killer. We turned her loose after a couple of hours."

Pete's phone dinged with a message. He looked at it. "This is not funny!" he shouted to the room. There was some laughter from the other end. Pete turned the phone so I could see an animated gif of a man throwing up. "Deputy Barf," it said.

"You did throw up on duty twice in one week. Besides, think about how much they must like you to give you a nickname."

"Yeah, right," he muttered good-naturedly. If you can't take a little ribbing, you're not going to last long in law enforcement. Pete had been on the giving end of more than a few jokes himself. "So, in complete confidence, Shantel told me you're coming back full time."

I rolled my eyes. "I haven't even talked to Dad yet. He's going to have more than a little to say about it."

"It's not going to make you jump through too many hoops. He just managed to fill one of the investigator positions and he still has two patrol positions open."

"Pete, you should have learned by now that Dad will do whatever the hell he wants to do."

"Have you seen the press conference that he and Tolland did this morning?" Pete asked. I hadn't. "He's in a good mood, and you and I are on the most favored list. Honestly, I should go in and ask for a raise."

"We'll see. But I wouldn't be surprised if I end up filling one of those patrol positions. Do we know who he hired as an investigator?"

Pete looked at me with a smirk. "I shouldn't tell you. It might make you change your mind about coming back."

"He didn't."

"He did. Darlene Marks starts the first of March."

"That woman pointed a gun at me," I grumbled.

"She did find you in a room with a murdered man. Probably why your dad hired her. Not because she held a gun on you, but because she was willing to see the possibility of an officer being a bad guy. Shows she thinks outside the box."

"Thanks a lot."

"Well, if you're going to beg for your job back, now is as good a time as any."

"You're probably right. Maybe I'll get a little sympathy for the beating I took." I touched my side and groaned.

Dad's assistant smiled at me as I approached his office. I could tell that Shantel had told everyone I was coming back. She had probably been afraid that I'd change my mind, so she took the precaution of making it general knowledge. I sighed and asked if I could see the sheriff.

"Sure. I think he's been waiting for you."

I went into Dad's office and stopped when I saw Mauser. I wasn't sure that I could take one of his enthusiastic greetings in the shape I was in. To my shock, Mauser got up, shuffled over to me and leaned gently against my hip.

"Damn you," I told him. "You get all sweet like this and I'll decide I actually like you." I gave him a vigorous ear rub, even though the movement sent pain running across my ribs. "Okay, that's enough, big guy, I don't like you that much." Mauser circled a couple of times and laid back down next to Dad's desk.

Dad was sorting papers on his desk and pretending to ignore me. The papers looked like applications. He looked up and tried to keep from smiling.

"What do you want?" he asked as gruffly as he could manage. He didn't invite me to sit down.

"I'm sure you've already heard it through the grapevine. I'd like to come back full time," I said flatly.

He leaned back in his chair and looked up at me.

"I know you're a good deputy. I know you're a better investigator than you are a patrol officer. And you are a very good investigator. A little raw around the edges, and I think you get by on luck too often, but I can't argue with the results. What I want to know is, are you going to be committed to the job? I realize you became a deputy because I asked you to. Now you're asking me if you can come back to the job. I'm willing to take you back, but on one condition. You have to be able to look me in the eye and tell me that this is what you want. That you aren't doing this for me, or just to have a job, or because you can't think of anything else to do. No, I want you to tell me you're doing this because you *want* to be an investigator." He paused. "Can you do that?"

I felt like I was getting married. Of course, the joke is that cops are married to the job, so maybe it did take that kind of commitment. I looked him in the eye.

"Yes. I want to be a deputy."

He looked down at Mauser. "Mauser gave you a paws up, so…" He stared back at me for a minute and then gave me one of his very rare, ear-to-ear smiles. "Fine. You did great work catching Winston and not getting killed. And as a reward for that, I'm going to let you come back as an investigator. Honestly, it wouldn't be fair to patrol to put you back on the streets."

Wow, I thought, *brought back without some cruel punishment.* He really was in a good mood. But then the other shoe fell.

"However," he went on, "you won't be Pete's partner. You'll be teamed up with our newest investigator, Darlene Marks. You can help her transition from the Calhoun Police Department."

My mouth dropped open. "This is punishment for having quit," I blurted out before I could stop myself.

"You are very perceptive. That's what makes you a good investigator. Now, get out of here before I change my mind about hiring you back."

Stunned, I turned around and walked out. *How could things be worse?* I thought. Then I bumped into Julio as I was walking back to my old desk.

"Hey, Larry, glad you're back," he said.

I nodded, still trying to comprehend what had just happened to me.

"Guess who's back in town," he said. "Your looney ex-girlfriend Marcy. I just saw her at the Fast Mart."

Oh, crap.

Larry Macklin returns in:

March's Luck
A Larry Macklin Mystery–Book 5

Here's a preview:

I walked into the sheriff's office on a Tuesday morning and waved to Dill Kirby, the semi-retired sergeant working the front desk. He gave me a broad smile.

"Mornin', Larry! She beat ya in," he said loudly and laughed wickedly at my expense.

"Thanks, old man," I threw back at him, but he just shook his head and chuckled.

I walked down the hall and turned the corner into the large open area that housed the criminal investigations department. Adams County is small and rural, so there were only ten desks in the room. Mine sat between the desk of my old partner, Pete Henley, and that of my new partner, Darlene Marks. Darlene was at her desk, staring at her monitor. A big mug of coffee from the Fast Mart sat by her elbow, while her leg tapped quickly up and down.

I tried to be inconspicuous as I walked over to my desk. All I wanted was a couple of minutes to sit down and look over any reports that had been assigned to me from the night before and to generally wake up. I knew that I didn't stand a chance.

"Morning, rookie!" Darlene said cheerfully. Way too cheerfully for eight-thirty in the morning.

"Why do you call me that? I've been working here for nearly seven years. You're the one that started barely a week ago," I grumbled at her. We'd been over this ground before.

"I've been in law enforcement for ten years, pal. Your dad's just got you showing me around. It's not like you're my field training officer."

"You're not my FTO either, so stop calling me rookie," I said.

"You have got to learn to take a joke. Everyone should have a nickname. Like your old partner, Deputy Barf," she said lightly.

I looked longingly over at Pete's desk. He was probably eating breakfast at the Donut Hole right now. He had never come in and called me names before nine o'clock in the morning. I missed working with Pete a lot.

"We've got some doozies from last night," Darlene went on. "Here's one we can work on together," she said, handing me a copy of a report from patrol.

Lt. Johnson came in around seven every morning and went through the previous night's reports and assigned them to investigators. Easy cases could be handled by one investigator, but for something more serious we'd team up with our partners and work them together. Since Darlene had become my partner, I'd found that I was willing to work on some pretty big cases by myself. But if she asked for my help on a case, I really couldn't refuse.

"Somebody stole a backhoe. Brand new. Thing's worth twenty-five thousand."

"That's less than some cars," I said, not wanting to be drawn into it.

"Yeah, but they almost ran over some homeless guy on their way out of the yard with it. Knocked him down. Could have killed him." Darlene got excited easily. Though, looking over the report, I had to admit that we could bring some pretty serious charges against the thief.

The homeless man had been taken to a hospital in Tallahassee. "Contacting the hospital would be one of the first steps," I said reluctantly. Glancing over at Darlene, I saw that she was already on the phone. She mouthed: *Calling the hospital.* I sighed and went back to looking over my own assignments.

An hour later we pulled into the parking lot of Mill's Lumber and Supply. They were the local John Deere dealership and it was their backhoe that had gone missing.

The manager, Dave Rudd, took us out back.

"Damned thing. I got a call from the alarm company about two o'clock. Now, that ain't unusual, stupid thing goes off a couple times a month. Can't get them to fix it right. Anyway, that's why I wasn't too excited. I got dressed, with my wife cussin' up a storm about being woke up again, and headed out to my truck. That's when I got a call from one of your deputies that the fence was all tore to hell and some guy was hurt. Well, I didn't know who he was talking about. We don't have a night watchman or anything. Of course, now that I think about it, a night watchman might not be a bad idea."

Dave kept talking all the way to the back lot. I listened with half an ear while Darlene took meticulous notes. Not easy since she was walking too.

"He cut our chain, then backed up and hooked his truck up to the trailer. Guess we shouldn't have left it on the trailer, but who the hell would think someone would cut through the lock?" Dave said, shaking his head.

We looked at the chain and lock. The chain was heavy-duty, but the lock, not so much. The thief had cut the lock off and was in like Flynn.

"I'll be glad to come out and give your place a security check," Darlene told Dave. They wandered off, talking about all the problems of securing a large site, while I looked around the grounds. Attached to the report was a picture of the backhoe and trailer that were stolen. From where I stood, I could see at least three pieces of heavy equipment that looked more expensive and just as easy to steal.

"Why do you think they took that backhoe?" I asked Rudd. He stopped and looked at me, slightly puzzled.

"You know, I wondered that myself."

"The report said they also broke into your office. Where is that?" Darlene asked him.

"Over here," he said, leading us to a small annex built onto the store with a sign over the door that read "John

Deere Sales". He pointed to the door, which looked like someone had just taken a crowbar and levered the door open. Sykes, the deputy responding, had dusted the door and the office for prints. With small cases, our deputies often do the evidence collection themselves.

"They took the keys. In fact, they took a lot of keys," Dave said, sounding a bit tired. "I'm going to have to get replacement keys for all of the equipment they didn't steal." A thought occurred to him. "You don't think they're planning on coming back for the other rigs, do you?"

"No. I'm sure they took all the keys 'cause they didn't know which set went to the one they were going to steal," I reassured him.

"The good news is that probably means it's not an inside job," Darlene said, making notes. *Points to her*, I thought.

"Ohhhh, I see. Because if it was one of our guys, he'd know which set of keys went with which backhoe. Yeah, gee, I hadn't even thought it could have been one of our employees. Wow, that *is* good news."

"Interesting," Darlene said. She had an irritating habit of making you ask what she was talking about, but this time I was on top of it.

"You're right," I told her. "The thief didn't ransack the office."

Dave looked back and forth between Darlene and me. I explained, "That means our bad guy wasn't after money. Which was also my point about the backhoe he stole. It wasn't the most valuable one on your lot."

Dave nodded thoughtfully.

"Gooseneck trailer, right?" I asked.

"Yep, you don't want something that big and heavy hanging off your bumper," he said, falling quickly into the cadence of a sales pitch.

I held up my hand and called dispatch, asking if they had any reports of a truck being stolen in the last forty-eight hours.

"Bingo," I said after getting contact info from the

dispatcher. "A dually was stolen from a farm south of town last night."

"The plot thickens," Darlene said with way too much enthusiasm.

Before we left I turned to Dave. "This may be a stupid question, but what would someone do with that particular piece of equipment?"

"Dig a hole, fill in a hole, or both," he answered, eyebrows raised. I nodded. *Stupid question.*

After we'd been out and talked with the farmer whose truck was stolen, I was forced to admit to myself—not to Darlene, but just to myself—that this case was a lot more interesting than I'd thought it would be when I read the report.

"The thief had to know where that truck was," Darlene said as I drove. We'd decided to go to the Donut Hole for lunch. With Winston's Grill closed after the owner had turned out to be a homicidal maniac, the Donut Hole had ramped up their lunch menu, adding wraps and more sandwiches.

"Yep," I agreed. The farm was pretty far out of town. "Which means that's probably our best chance. There has to be a connection. Our crook could be a family member, friend, neighbor or an ex-employee."

"Or possibly he spotted the truck in town and decided that was the one he wanted, then followed the truck out to the farm."

"Maybe, but he'd be taking a chance. How would he know that the owner left the keys in the truck?" I asked. Though, honestly, that wasn't as rare on a farm as it would be in town. A farmer could have several farmhands that might need to use the truck, so sometimes it was just easier to leave the keys in the vehicle so that anyone that needed it didn't have to hunt up the person with the keys.

We took our sandwiches and sat at one of the picnic tables outside the small restaurant. With Darlene eating and not talking, I enjoyed my lunch and the quiet, watching a steady stream of folks come and go. The loss of Winston's had been a godsend for the Donut Hole.

The weather was perfect. The sun was shining in a clear blue sky and a cool breeze blew through the trees. In north Florida the worst of the winter weather is usually over by mid-March. There can still be the occasional freeze or days of rain, but most days are like this, making you want to spend them lying in the grass and staring up at the sky.

The peace of the afternoon was shattered when I heard the screech of brakes. I looked up to see a small, bright red car make a sharp turn into the parking lot. The driver was short and something about the profile set the hairs on the back of my neck on end. The car slammed to a stop and the door was open before the vehicle had stopped rocking back and forth.

"Damn it!" I blurted out involuntarily, looking for some way to escape. Darlene just stared at the wild-eyed, black-haired woman who came stomping over to our table.

"You haven't answered any of my texts," Marcy Pike loudly accused me.

I stood up, facing my ex-girlfriend. "Just calm down. I don't have to answer your texts," I said reasonably. "Besides, I haven't gotten most of them because I blocked you after I got the first one."

Her face turned a dangerous, fiery red. "You son of a—" Surprisingly, she stopped herself. "Look, I just want to talk to you." Marcy had turned the volume on her voice down by half, trying to sound sane.

I looked around at the dozen people, including Darlene, who'd stopped eating in order to watch the show. "Fair enough," I said, turning back to her. "Let's go over to your car."

One of the things that galled Marcy the most was someone being rational, but she seemed to swallow her desire for battle and nodded.

I took out my phone as we walked to her car. "Let me

finish this text," I said when we stopped. On my phone I typed out: *watch us. if things get ugly come break it up,* and sent the text to Darlene.

"Are you done?" Marcy asked with narrowed eyes as I put my phone away.

"Sorry," I said, trying to throw some water on whatever fire she wanted to get started. "I heard your dad's been sick. I hope he gets better soon."

"He's pretty bad off. He's in hospice now," Marcy said and, for a moment, there was real emotion in her voice. But it was all gone by the time she spat out the next sentence. "Look, I need any of my stuff that you still have."

"What stuff? We lived together, like, nine years ago," I reminded her.

"I know I left some stuff when I moved out," Marcy said accusingly.

"Maybe. I don't know. Some junk, yeah. But I've moved twice since then." The first time I'd moved after she left me was because I was afraid she'd come back, but I decided pointing that out wouldn't help the situation.

"Are you telling me you threw it out?" It was like watching a locomotive start moving down the track. I could see the pressure building up behind her eyes.

"Yes. I don't think there was anything but some old makeup, maybe some towels, an old pair of sandals. Literally just junk," I told her, trying to think of anything else she might have left and what she could possibly want with it now.

"That was my stuff," she said, glaring at me.

"Well, maybe you should have gotten it when you moved out," I answered, exasperated.

I watched as she calculated how far to take this. Suddenly, her eyes shifted. "Yeah, okay. You're saying you don't have anything of mine?"

"That's right." I knew that she'd shifted into plotting mode. Not a good sign, but I couldn't do anything about it.

"Fine, be that way." Marcy threw open the door to her

car, trying to hit me with it, and dropped into the driver's seat. I moved away quickly, knowing that if she had the opportunity she'd run me over as she left the parking lot. From a safe distance, I watched her spin out of the driveway.

A boxy sedan that I recognized pulled in seconds after Marcy took off down the road. "Was that who I think it was?" Pete asked me after he got out.

"I don't want to talk about it," I said good-naturedly.

"I understand that, brother." Pete and I hadn't known each other back when I was dating Marcy, but he'd heard the stories, both from me and from mutual friends. He looked over at the Donut Hole. "I sure miss Winston's." He held up his hand to stop me. "Not Winston himself. That guy can rot in hell."

"How's Mary doing?" I asked.

"Confused. Trying to understand everything." Pete shrugged. "It has to be tough when you find out your loving father is a serial killer."

"You ready to go, rookie?" Darlene asked, coming up behind me.

I rolled my eyes so that only Pete could see. "Talk to you later," I told him, longing for the days when we were partners.

I'd just pulled the car out of the driveway when the dispatch radio cut in to tell us that Sergeant Will Toomey was requesting our presence out at Parrish Farm, but not giving any details. Whenever possible, our dispatchers tried to be discreet. Even in this day and age of two hundred TV channels and the Internet, a few folks in the county still had police band scanners. And they also had cell phones; if they heard something really exciting going down on the radio, they'd text it to half the county.

If Toomey wanted us, then it was important. Once I was headed that way, I called him on my phone.

"Possibly an accident, but equally likely it's a homicide. And no one is going to be happy about the victim," Toomey said sadly. "It's Mr. Parrish himself."

Damn it, I thought. Hank Parrish was one of the richest farmers in the county and a model human being. More personally, he'd been a great friend to my dad, helping him with his first election to sheriff and supporting him ever since.

Parrish land covered thousands of acres spread over a large part of the county. Toomey gave me directions to a hay field a quarter mile from the main house. I told him we'd be there in fifteen minutes and hung up.

ACKNOWLEDGMENTS

A big thank you goes to my beta readers, Sam Azner and Liane Schrader, for their comments and encouragement. And thanks to everyone who has read this series so far. I am humbled by how well it has done and I'm glad that others seem to enjoy reading this series as much as I enjoy writing it.

As always, I have to recognize the amazing and constant support and encouragement I've received from H. Y. Hanna. Her advice has been invaluable and I firmly believe that her cover designs have played a big part in the series' success. Words cannot express my appreciation for all her help.

Good fortune smiled on me when I met a woman who could be my friend, my editor and my wife. Many things in my life, including this series, could not be accomplished without Melanie by my side.

Original Cover Design by H. Y. Hanna
Paperback Cover Design by Robin Ludwig Design Inc.
www.gobookcoverdesign.com

ABOUT THE AUTHOR

A. E. Howe lives and writes on a farm in the wilds of north Florida with his wife, horses and more cats than he can count. He received a degree in English Education from the University of Georgia and is a produced screenwriter and playwright. His first published book was *Broken State*; the Larry Macklin Mysteries is his first series and he has plans for more. Howe is also the co-host of the "Guns of Hollywood" podcast, part of the Firearms Radio Network. When not writing or podcasting, Howe enjoys riding, competitive shooting and working on the farm.

Made in United States
North Haven, CT
10 May 2023

36423058R00139